D1435912

Tales from Webster's:

The Verminous Resuscitator and

The Monsignor in the Zoot Suit

John Shea

Copyright © 2017 John Shea
All rights reserved, including electronic text

ISBN 13: 978-1-60489-188-1, hardcover
ISBN 13: 978-1-60489-189-8, trade paper
ISBN: 1-60489-188-2 hardcover
ISBN: 1-60489-189-0 trade paper
Library of Congress Control Number 2017942048
Printed on acid-free paper
by Publishers Graphics
Printed in the United States of America

Hardcover binding by: Heckman Bindery
Typesetting and page layout: Sarah Coffey
Proofreading: Joe Taylor, Shelby Parrish, Sarah Coffey, Patricia Taylor
Cover design: Abby Ames

Cover photos of Daniel Webster

The Tartt First Fiction Award is sponsored by
the President's Office at UWA.

For Karen, Zach, and Molly

This is a work of fiction:
any resemblance
to persons living or dead is coincidental.

Livingston Press is part of The University of West Alabama,
and thereby has non-profit status.
Donations are tax-deductible:
brothers and sisters, we need 'em.

first edition
6 5 4 3 3 2 1

Author's Note

The "tales from Webster's" are a literary form I invented. The bolded key words on the left of the page are consecutive entries in *Webster's New World Dictionary*, Second College Edition (World Publishing Company, 1970). The text on the right is my connective tissue linking those words into a narrative, scene, or evocation of personality. The tale is read the customary way, beginning at the highest point and moving from left to right. There must be at least five key words; and the linking text is no more than 50 words long.

Acknowledgments

"paramount – paraphrase" appeared in *The Ampersand Review*, June 2012.

"respiratory system – resuscitator" appeared in *Literal Latte*, Fall 2009.

"abecedarian — abiding", "strabismus — straightaway", "Hieronymus — highborn", "paramount — paraphrase", "weapon — weather" and "Chablis — chador" appeared in *Tartts Seven*, 2016

Table of Contents

Hancock – handicap

In which a visitor has dire plans for a global conference.

journey – jovial

In which the similarity between life and football is reaffirmed.

mostly – mother

In which a shady job in Mosul turns even more deadly.

offend – office boy

In which commentators offer expert opinions on football strategy – and war.

Chablis – chador

In which some society folk say some gossipy things about other society folk.

icicle – icosahedron

In which the spurned Professor Brown plots his revenge on academe.

swashbuckler – swath

In which the government official parries an angry protestor.

respiratory system – resuscitator

In which an antiquarian uses the dark arts to summon a baleful god.

dominance – Dominic

In which some principles of war are expounded in a home setting.

Eckhart – ecstatic

In which Mr. Shaw discovers some frightening implications of the "need to know" principle.

night life – nigrescent

In which a vampire muses about what he observes when the sun goes down.

yarrow – Yazoo

In which we learn how a sailor's life began in flight from a flashing blade.

inescapable – inexplicable

In which a spin doctor explains exactly where the president stands on certain key issues.

Lohengrin – lollygag

In which randy Lois teaches the bashful knight a thing or two.

Nebraska – negotiation

In which a well-known CEO writes about his rise to success and the travails overcame.

obliquity – oboe

In which Riley's anti-capitalist terrorism backfires.

rattrap – Rawalpindi

In which a restaurant critic begs to differ with the positive reviews of Chez Veronique.

where – whicker

In which two travelers vigorously debate where they're going.

usual – Utopian

In which an author heatedly responds to a reviewer, and vice versa.

delicate – della Robbia

In which strangers meet, dally energetically, and are interrupted by a voice from beyond.

identical twins – ideomotor

In which a retired researcher recalls the good old days of unhampered investigations.

fledgling – fleet

In which a clever street urchin displays some dubious skills.

glyptograph – goat

In which a world-famous symbologist is presented with another astonishing case.

Monsignor – monstrance

In which a priest in the confessional struggles against temptation.

Kt – kudzu

In which a rock band, on its world tour, wonders about some of the venues they're playing.

memento – Memphis

In which a late friend's collection brings much more than expected.

year – Yeats

In which a husband recalls – and is astonished by – his early passion.

Zarathustra – zebec

In which her new zeal to continue her education is not well received.

nocturnal – nodding acquaintance

In which a poet provides an autobiographical sketch.

Fichte – fiddle-faddle

In which a philosophy student and his girlfriend argue about the essence of fiction.

dit – dithyramb

In which the lover discovers his beloved's less-than-loving ways.

career woman – carhop

In which Mira considers the costs of doing business.

driving – drop

In which Clarke – rich, connected, and unscrupulous – makes a wrong turn in his Jaguar.

ill-boding – ill-treat

In which Smith meets Smyth, and the meeting soon sours.

verminous – vernal

In which two e-mails from Vermont express rather different opinions of the state.

accompanist – accordion

In which two not-so-clever thieves plan a jewel heist.

Lisle – literate

In which a man is interrogated about his possible appearance on a possible list.

fearsome – feather

In which a fabled baseball slugger is challenged to a home run contest by a deli worker.

aghast – agleam

In which a scion of a prominent family reveals a new source of income.

Namaqualand – Namibia

In which Joe McCoy doesn't get to put the new guy at the office in his place.

undesigning – undone

In which Mlle. Brie attempts to correct the Senator's terrible French accent.

Zephyrus – Zeus

In which a German spy zeppelin ventures where another nation does not want it to go.

Pushtu – puss

In which a compelling case is made for a muscle-building product.

macumba – madhouse

In which Henry gradually falls under the spell of his wife's magical perfume.

viceroy – vichyssoise

In which Inspector Maggio interrupts the viceroy's important meeting.

dread – dredge

In which our unpopular hero daydreams about a life of adventure and romance.

Vaal – vacuum tube

In which a family's vacation goes horribly – and fantastically – awry.

Hindustan – hip

In which a veteran diplomat imparts some advice to a neophyte.

Jocelin – joggle

In which our narrator helps out a young woman teased by frat brothers.

quoit – q.y.

In which a trial appears in danger of veering off course.

smidgen – smithereens

In which the don receives a hospital visitor up to no good.

Quai d'Orsay – Quaker

In which two people of power – French and American – understand each other.

ungenerous – ungrammatical

In which we are privy to the hidden thoughts of two teachers.

regicide – region

In which 007 gets his next assignment.

xanthous – xebec

In which tired travelers reach the fabled city of Xanthus – which wasn't their destination.

Abaddon – abbess

In which a grim angel takes a brief leave of hell to see what's going on above.

orientation – Orion

In which an inexperienced man goes seeking worldly experience, gingerly.

man jack – manner

In which the Congressional freshmen are given fair warning.

knout – knucklehead

In which identical twins prove not to have the right stuff for a questionable experiment.

torso – totem

In which a rich and attractive woman suspects she is being pursued . . . but for what?

lycanthrope – Lycia

In which a man with wolfish traits ponders his place in the world.

reiterate – rejuvenate

In which an author declaims the agony and ecstasy – and agony once more – of writing.

badly – baggy

In which a lovesick chap tries to forget – on Baffin Island and then Manhattan.

zoot suit – zowie

In which the keeper of the tales receives a strange visit from the future.

Tales from Webster's:
The Verminous Resuscitator and
The Monsignor in the Zoot Suit

abecedarian — abiding

Welcome, friends, to this bold

a•be•ce•dar•i•an

undertaking. I've worked long and hard on it, night after cruel night, wrestling with a slippery muse, while you, no doubt, were

a•bed

or relaxing with a gin and tonic some-where near a soothing oceanfront or a grove of whispering pines. I, on the other hand, have suffered the fiery torments of

A•bed•ne•go

, and I'm still waiting for a savior like Daniel to deliver me. I speak, please note, metaphorically. But I've gone

a•beg•ging

for a wise and intrepid audience. Is there an

A•bel

among you, perhaps, who will read and treasure my work? But maybe Abel was not the best choice – slain by his own brother. Well, then, is there a broad-minded philosopher like, say,

Ab•é•lard

who will find my tales to be delightful and . . . wait! He lived a troubled life, lost his lover, became a hermit, was charged with heresy. Forget him. Let me rest under the shade of this fine

a•bele while I think. I don't want to give you
the wrong impression, that reading the
Tales from Webster's will lead to great
woes. Not at all! But I admit you won't
find anything about

A•bel•i•an groups in these pages, because, Lord
knows, I've forgotten just about
all I knew – or half-knew – about math.
And the Tales may not bring you up to
date on the hot tourist spots of

Ab•er•deen , either. But let's face it, even an

Ab•er•deen An•gus should find plenty of aesthetic excitement in these pages. And if you are not
entertained, enlightened, and quickened,
perhaps it's because of an

ab•er•rant gene, some tiny difference in the six
billion nucleotides in your body.
Gee, I hope that's not the case. I may
be on shaky ground here, but you might
be able to minimize the results of the

ab•er•ra•tion by reading the complete Tales two or
three times through. Your consciousness
might be expanded. It might even help
to buy copies and send them to friends
and relatives. Far be it from me to

a•bet any kind of uncertain scheme, but I can
assure you that if you bought several
copies of the Tales from Webster's, I, for
one, would be very happy. But let's
hold that idea in

a•bey•ance for the present. Like you, I tend to

2

ab•hor	solicitations, pleas for money, aggressive marketing. I suspect, too, that you and I also share an
ab•hor•rence	for violent computer games, dishonest politicians, and flip flops worn anywhere but at the beach, where they belong. . . . Oh, you're not sure that you find the frightening rise of flip flops
ab•hor•rent	? Very well. Just don't expect any positive treatment of flip flops in this collection. In the meantime, I, the author, will
a•bide	, waiting for the readers that I know are out there. Handsome ones, elegant ones, with a twinkle of wit in their eyes. Eager to search out the new and unusual. Ready to laugh and marvel. My faith is
a•bid•ing	. And now excuse me while I go check on the proper pronunciation of Abednego.

puppy love —— purebred

The last thing Harry wanted was to bring disgrace to his father, the Empire, and the princely state of India in which he was living. But Sir Giles was wrong – it was not a case of

puppy love   that could be forgotten after some gin or even a night with a discreet courtesan as arranged by his father. No, Anju was much more than that to him. So Harry told Sir Giles he'd sleep in the

pup tent   that night, away from the huge house, because he was "in no state to be around people." That was true enough; but Harry had more on his mind. Almost every

pu•ra•na   Anju had read to him was filled with heroes who defied convention. Why should he shrink from his destiny? As the night dwindled, Harry crept out of the tent. He was nearly

pur•blind   with excitement and, it must be said, his father's port. He thought of the famous lovers of the past – Romeo and Juliet, Abélard and Heloise, the sad tale of Dido and Aeneas that had inspired

Pur•cell   to his finest music. As the moon persisted in blinking and wavering, Harry made his way stealthily to the rajah's palace. He'd come with some items in case he met a guard and had to

4

pur•chase   his way onto the grounds, including the gold watch Sir Giles had given him for finishing at Harrow. More moonlight that would not behave properly. All at once, he saw that Anju had defied

pur•dah   and was waiting for him in the shadows of the palace's eastern wall! Then he saw who was with her: her father the rajah. As guards seized him, he heard her cry, "I told him our love was

pure   !" The next day, hunched on the deck of the steamship as it left port, he recalled the rajah's words: "Count yourself blessed that my daughter's plea softened my heart. I'd have had eight

pure•bred   stallions of my cavalry tear you apart." But as Harry bowed his head, he could not imagine a feeling worse than what racked him now.

Amon-Re — amort

Some people worship Christ, some

A•mon-Re , but to be frank I prefer

a•mon•til•la•do . Call me

a•mor•al , then. I shan't dispute you. But I will follow that damn

am•o•ret•to , Eros, anywhere. Yes, I own to the title of

am•o•rist , with no shame when passion enflames me. I'd follow my object of desire to the desert of the Hottentot, the frozen wastes of the Lapp, or the dreaded home of the

Am•o•rite , if such there still be in the world. And she, no doubt, my Helen, my Dido, would be as

am•o•rous as I. We would disport, frolic, with no other cares. . . . What's that? You ask about honor, or

a•mor pat•ri•ae , or the greater good? Fie! The universe has no place for such

a•mor•phous abstractions. Self-deceptions, that's all. Life is brief. Forces conspire to frustrate us. Revel now before you are all

a•mort , my dear fellow.

strabismus — straightaway

stra•bis•mus

At the doorway he pauses, his tall figure now more stooped as he prepares to make his retirement remarks, a touch of

as he blinks while the flashes go off. Not that he's not used to being the center of attention. For decades, his students have admired his allusions to that old Greek historian,

Stra•bo

, or chuckled while he retold a few irreverent tales from Lytton

Stra•chey

, those too risqué to be in the Victorian book. She sees he's clutching the violin case, as usual. Now he enters, as well-wishers wish him well. All well and good. But is "the Old

Strad

," as he oh-so-casually referred to it, actually in the case? That time she had the tutorial, he had some other things inside. Unguents. Opium. Pills. Devices. But first he tried to

strad•dle

her. Oh, she fought him off, scratching his shocked face. Why else had she come, after all, but to please him? What would Signor

Stra•di•va•ri

have thought? His instrument used as a prop, a lure, by an artist, professor, . . . and predator. If his damn

Strad•i•var•i•us	had been there, she would have taken a hammer to it. Not that she carried one in her purse, but she'd have made do with something else. Later, she wished she could
strafe	him, cut him down to size, force him to listen to all he had done to her. And to how many other young women? And force the dean, Dr.
Straf•ford	, to listen as well. No doubt the dean had tried to downplay "what they thought had happened" when a student would
strag•gle	into his office and tearfully explain. "Are you sure? Could you have misinterpreted what he said?" Or did? And some later time, another, with a similar story, her eyes moist, her hair
strag•gly	? Psychosis? Or a spurned lover's revenge? Today, years later, she is determined to look him
straight	in the eye. No doubt he will not remember – or pretend not to. Just as he probably pretended to play a violin while planning his next volume of lapidary prose. But another woman, approaching at a
straight angle	, confronts him first. She appears to be a professor of the college. Well dressed. No sign of fear or anger. But calmly she slams him in the face,
straight-arm	, knocking him back. He reels. The violin case drops. There is a sudden silence

8

in the crowded room. She moves toward the door, and a line opens

straight•a•way   for her to pass. Someone begins to clap. Then another. Then more. A woman professor tears off her school pin and flings it in his direction. After all this time, a gesture. And perhaps more.

Garland — garni

Old Miss Turner closed the ledger. "Well, that's tonight's tally, Mary. Off you go, but be careful! These horrible events . . ." Mary

Gar•land waved her off. "I'll be fine, Miss Turner. I'm just going 'round the corner." "But it's already pitch black. Do me this one favor, then, and wear the

gar•lic wreath around your neck." "Oh, Miss Turner! I'll stink to high heaven!" "Better that than filling a fresh grave, don't you think, Mary?" Wrapping her worn

gar•ment about her, Mary hurried outside into the heavy fog. Another evening's work, long and hard, but she was determined to

gar•ner the funds she needed to move herself and her ailing father to the countryside. Sighing, she walked down the street, away from the light. In the darkness, a man with

gar•net lips fell into step a few yards behind her. His tread was almost silent. But not quite. Mary slowed her pace, tilting her head to listen. Nervously, she touched the crucifix with the

gar•net stone, a gift of her dead mother. Oh, for a revolver instead! she thought, quickening her pace again. "Yes, she is right to worry," murmured Sebastian

Gar•nett , the late Lord Carfax. With sudden speed, he was upon her, throwing her cloak aside and showing his gleaming teeth. Then he saw the wreath . . . and fled. "I dearly love my meat

gar•ni ," he laughed, later, hidden again in the fog, "but not, alas, like that."

weapon —— weather

"Do not be swayed by the opinions of the others, the deceivers," said the president of Iran, peering out over the vast crowd in the plaza. "Remember, he who holds the

weap•on makes the history. For much too long, our nation and those who share our faith have been scolded: Israel must be a sovereign state, because of the Holocaust. So says the

weap•on•eer , smug behind his array of nuclear devices. And we bowed down, because we were powerless, even though we knew there was never a Holocaust. But now we have the

weap•on•ry , too, and we can speak the truth: Israel is an outlaw state, founded on lies." He withdrew to thunderous applause. But the

wear of the day had taken its toll. Soon he was curled up in his office for a nap before his next address.

Someone was shaking him. The room was dim, smelly. "What are you doing? Fool! You must

wear your shirt or they will beat you to death at once! Here, put this on." A stoop-shouldered man in a striped uniform handed him a threadbare striped shirt that seemed scarcely

12

wear•a•ble	. Confused, the president took it, then flung it away. He had seen the tattoo of blue numbers on the stranger's forearm. "A Jew!" "Oh, your insight is truly impressive . . . but I feel the
wear and tear	too much to stand here exchanging pleasantries. And you can be a living Jew if you put on your uniform – or a dead Jew if you don't, and the guards see you." He shrugged, rubbing his
wea•ri•ful	eyes. "You young fellows may feel
wea•ri•less	, but a few beatings by our hosts will soon change that." He picked up the shirt with evident
wea•ri•ness	and held it out to the president. The president shook his head angrily. "This little performance is clumsy and very
wear•ing	. What lunatic put you up to this? I'll have him flogged for this
wea•ri•some	prank!" The older man sighed. "Look, my friend, after so many months of sorrow and pain, so many months of cleaning up after my brutal captors, my feelings are
wear•proof	, but don't try this nonsense on those guards. They'll be only too happy to drag you over to the delousing chambers." "Oh, yes, the gas chambers that never existed." "I'm too
wea•ry	to debate you." Suddenly, the door was

flung open, and three guards with rifles and clubs entered. "Too much noise, Blum," said one. Then, with a curse, he grabbed the president around the

wea•sand , nearly choking him. "This one – who is he? Where is his uniform? What is his serial number?" Blum shrugged. "I'm afraid he's a little simple, sir. Please spare him." "Ha! Another

wea•sel trying to duck his job. We'll show him." "He suffered a blow to the head, sir," said Blum, bowing low. "Have pity, please." The guard knocked Blum to the ground. "Enough of your

weasel words , Jew. You always stick together, don't you?" Stunned, the president could not find words as they seized him and marched him outside the hut into the twilight. The

weath•er was brutally cold. The president stared at their weapons. A vicious wind swept past. He almost wished he had taken the shirt from the old Jew.

14

Hieronymus — highborn

Hi•er•on•y•mus

hi•er•o•phant

hi•fa•lu•tin

hi•fi

Hig•gin•son

hig•gle

hig•gle•dy-pig•gle•dy

"Boss? We got the story. It's definitely front-page stuff, almost like something out of

Bosch. Yeah, there was the senator, all dolled up in a jeweled robe, presiding at the event like he was a goddamned

at the ancient mysteries, intoning some Semitic-sounding gibberish and giving some

spiel about the need for — hold on, I've got it in my notes — 'the corporeality of the adepts to be refreshed by the willing flesh of the catechumens.' Meanwhile the

is blaring. Reminded me a little of *Carmina Burana* or something, a lot of voices sounding ponderous and mysterious. Then Senator

steps up to the makeshift altar and selects one of the young women for what was quaintly called the ceremony. What? . . . Of course she was naked! But then they start to

and haggle. Seems she wants her job offer to be Congressional page signed by the senator then and there before she, quote, puts out. Then things start going real

, especially when Sandra Freemont — you know, the local leader of the Young

Republicans — begins to complain about the

high cost of the booze that the adepts are now pouring over their naked bodies. At which point the would-be page tosses a

high•ball into Higginson's face, and, with a howl and a hard-on, he takes off after her like a

high•bind•er on the trail of a million-dollar bribe. It was a scary sight to see that much bare — but very

high•born — poundage in motion. A statement from his office? I wouldn't count on it."

laud — laundress

"As of now, the Sacred Confluence has found reason to

laud
most of the efforts of our covert exploratory force, as small as it is. My own mention, last eventide, of the historical Archbishop

Laud
was a regrettable misstep. I had not known that he had been executed for treason by the English authorities, and thus my attempted humoristic saying failed. However

laud•a•ble
our efforts at learning the history and culture of this planet, we must be precise. And when Three, at the same convivial assemblage of natives, requested

laud•a•num
for his refreshment, we were extremely fortunate that it was taken as a witticism. Remember: one cannot fail when asking for red wine or clear wine, after the sipping of which a brief

lau•da•tion
can be expressed. Learn, too, the athletic teams of these local inhabitants and issue

laud•a•to•ry
comments. But avoid becoming too engrossed, as it appears there are often fierce approvals and disapprovals of said athletes and teams. Seven invoked a certain Estée

Lau•der
, but she turned out to be something other than a highly recompensed sports figure. Again, be careful. A casual nod may

17

suffice in answer to many questions. And if uncertain,

laugh   , but only lightly, as if acknowledging one's narrow expertise. Alas, determining what is a grave matter and what is

laugh•a•ble   will take some time, and given the circumstances on our home planet, our time is not limitless. As well, when in the sanctuary, practice

laugh•ing   , which is important in social settings. The vocalizations should not be overly loud. Restrict the movements of the jaw muscles. We should investigate the substance known as

laughing gas   and determine whether it would be of use during our practice. Four had a narrow escape last eventide when he complimented the voice of Most Important Female, saying it was akin to that of a

laughing jackass   . I was able to soothe her feelings by explaining that Four had been struck on the head by a masked ruffian and was not himself. We must be careful! Let none of us become a

laugh•ing•stock   , which draws undue attention. It is acceptable to elicit what are known as titters or giggles, but too much

laugh•ter   can be counterproductive and may even raise suspicions. If a conversation with a native seems to be leading to dangers, change topics. Raise the matter of ectoplasm or the fish known as a

launce or the derivation of pi or the economy of the Australian port called

Laun•ces•ton or ask the native whether he or she has ever gone out to the depths of the sea in an engine-driven

launch and speared marlins or octopi or if he or she is intending to

launch a political campaign, which apparently happens very frequently in this sadly disunited planet. Our time for gathering information is nearly at an end, and soon we will return to our

launch•er . The Sacred Confluence has again emphasized that we must not miss the appointed time to gather at the

launch pad because there will be no variation in the scheduled departure. All of you know the

launch window . If, like our comrade Three, you have engrimed or splattered your Earth costuming, you must attempt to

laun•der it yourself using the tiny packets of soap placed in the hotel bathrooms. Or I gather that there is a site called a

Laun•der•ette where powerful machines will clean the apparel efficiently. Seven has asked about using a so-called

laun•dress to provide service, but it is safer not to involve a native, especially if questions are asked about the stains unfamiliar on Earth. When we return, things will be different. Quite different."

dismay — dispeople

dis•may

Ahura Mazda gave a great sigh of , shaking all the forests in the nearest continent and causing a few of the smaller rivers to jump their banks. Ahriman, about to

dis•mem•ber

a corporate attorney who had made some bad decisions in his miserable life, paused to listen. "And what could be bothering my colleague so much?" he asked himself. He made a gesture to

dis•miss

the bewildered attorney, who took the

dis•miss•al

as an act of god – as indeed it was – and dashed out on his bleeding feet into the desert wastes surrounding Ahriman's favorite summer home. A heartbeat later, Ahriman was giving a

dis•mis•sive

nod to the Titan who guarded Ahura Mazda's shimmering castle. No need to mount or

dis•mount

when you have the power of instant transport. Just before stepping over the threshold into Mazda's world, he made a mystical sign to

dis•na•ture

the lush valley behind him. "Still the same, eh, Ahriman," said Ahura Mazda, sighing again but less forcefully. "You can't help yourself." "Bosh, my friend. If you are the

20

Dis•ney	of the cosmos, then I'm the anti-Disney. It's what I do. And speaking of Disney, your place looks a little too much like that cutesy pastel castle in
Dis•ney•land	! Who does your design?" "Black leather, studs – who designs your clothes?" replied Ahura Mazda tartly. "But I have weightier things to contemplate." "Tax problems?" "No,
dis•o•be•di•ence	." "Wife Five through Wife Fifteen, I suppose?" "No, my wearisome colleague. I'm speaking of
dis•o•be•di•ent	humans. You create them, you set them up, you lay down just a few ground rules, and what's the first thing they do?" "Start worshipping me, like any right-thinking creature?" "No, they
dis•o•bey	, although worshipping you is part of it. Of course, they don't know your taste in clothing." "Well, what do you propose? As you know, I'm always ready to
dis•o•blige	you in any way possible and spread
dis•op•er•a•tion	where you have done your best to spread growth and progress and cooper- ation among your man-mites. My strength is
dis•or•der	, what some have called 'mere anarchy,' although from my perspective there's nothing mere about it." "No one has a higher opinion of you than you, that we know. But I've grown tired of

dis•or•dered   humans, greedily pursuing the wrong goals." "A wager, then. Let's take a closer look at one specimen. If he takes the wrong path, I win and get to destroy the whole vile,

dis•or•der•ly   race. If he acquits himself in your eyes, I'll saunter back to my desert retreat so you can bask in pride all by yourself." "We shall see." "That one, for example, hauled into the police station for

disorderly conduct   . Let's listen."

     "But I tell you, officers, I just had a bit too much to drink. How was I to know that my key wouldn't fit because it wasn't my house!" "It was a

disorderly house   , as my Aunt Phyllis used to say. A house of ill-repute." "There! What did I tell you? My own damn house is disorderly enough, what do I need some-one else's for?" The logic threatened to

dis•or•gan•ize   Sgt. Perkins's delicate scaffolding of thought. Meanwhile, the man whirled around, taking in the station's surroundings, and the motion threatened to

dis•o•ri•ent   him. "Whoa. My brain must be bubbling. Is there a plastic bag I can borrow?" "What do you need a plastic bag for?" asked the sergeant. A moment later, he wanted to

dis•own   his fellow human beings as he stepped back from the mess on the floor. "That's why. Oh, well, too late now." Sgt. Perkins sighed. "Don't mean to

dis•par•age   you and your fine family, but do you happen to recall where you live?" "No

dis•par•age•ment   taken!" replied the man brightly. Then he frowned. "There's been too much of that kind of garbage these days, let me tell you. Just this evening, I was fortunate enough to meet up with a rather

dis•pa•rate   group of individuals, all very good friends of mine, although at this point I'm rather fuzzy on whether we had met on previous occasions. And despite our

dis•par•i•t•y   , none of us had the least compunction about calling the other a raving jerk and a moronic ass. How do you like that? That's equality! That's . . . can you help me? I'm stuck. Can you

dis•part   my one leg from the other? They seem to be tangled somewhat. Bit dizzy. Mind if I take a seat?" "Not at all," replied Sgt. Perkins in a professional,

dis•pas•sion•ate   tone. He was still hoping to finish his shift and get home before supper got cold. So it would be nice – very nice – if he could work with

dis•patch   . He helped the drunk stagger to the old, wooden chair and looked up to see the

dis•patch•er   shaking his head grimly. The holding cell was rather full, wasn't it? "So you see, Mr. Policeman," said the man, as if they'd been continuing the conversation, "I have been sent to

dis•pel   your gloom. I bring joy wherever I go.
That's customarily with some money to
spend, but it appears that I do not have
any money to spend. Now that I think
about it, money is surely

dis•pen•sa•ble   , and we can all afford to live without it
every now and then. Which reminds me:
my employer notified me today that I,
too, was eminently dispensable. I was
on my way to the

dis•pen•sa•ry   to get some medicine for my daughter.
That's when things get a little hazy,
but it seems I spent those last dollars
on something else. Drink, I believe.
Funny how that happens under this cosmic

dis•pen•sa•tion   . Not the wisest move I've made." He
lowered his head, then looked around.
"Not the wisest." Sgt. Perkins sighed.
"Lucky for you, I'm a designated

dis•pen•sa•tor   in this part of town. Do you remember
how to get home?" "I think so," said the
man after a pause. "Do you remember
what medicine you need?" "I think so."
"Then let's stop at the

dis•pen•sa•to•ry   or clinic or whatever and see what we
can do." He helped the man to his feet,
nodded to the dispatcher, and walked
with him to the entrance.
          "There!" said Ahriman. "Time to

dis•pense   some justice, don't you think? To the
eternal fires with all of them! Your
drunkard wayward father is a disgrace –
but how perfect a representative of your
human flock! Let me be the

24

dis•pen•ser   of justice." "Your perspective is a little
off." "What nonsense! Allow me to

dis•peo•ple   the world of these miserable creatures,
done in by their exemplar!" "On the
contrary," said Ahura Mazda. "The exemplar was not the drunk but the policeman.
I think I'll give them more time."

"Thank you for coming — and a special thanks to Inspector March for allowing us to gather at the scene of the crime. It is

par•a•mount

for our purposes that we establish certain facts. Colonel Carter's Brazilian cook, Flor, was, it is now clear, also his

par•a•mour

. Thanks to our consul there, we have learned that she was forced to flee from her home in

Pa•ra•ná

because of some financial irregularities. Someone else in the colonel's household knew of her background, yet something did not fit: the knife used to kill him is a

pa•rang

, which is native *not* to South America but to Malaysia. More and more, it began to seem like an attempt to frame Flor. And Miss Carter's much-publicized

par•a•noi•a

began to seem a little overdone when she found the dead tarantula in her bed: would a true

par•a•noid

have run screaming into the parlor . . . *after* tying the laces of her sturdy black oxfords?" "But what about the ghost of the colonel?" asked Inspector March. "Ah, yes — the

par•a•nor•mal

! How boring life would be without it . . . but, I regret to say, it seems in this case merely a deceptive sideshow, much like the

par•a•nymph of ancient Greece, who accompanied the groom when he went to bring his wife home." "Enough empty erudition, Tyler," said Sims, patting Miss Carter's hand. "Explain the sighting on the

par•a•pet ." "Of the dead man, you mean? Oddly enough, the note he left accusing Flor bore his signature — quite realistic — but it lacked one thing: the colonel's characteristic

par•aph under the second *r*. In other words, a forgery. Then, we discovered a curious old photograph hidden among the colonel's wartime

par•a•pher•na•li•a , showing his sister, Miss Carter . . . and a certain penniless Londoner — now known as Crispin Sims!" Inspector March leaped to his feet. "Then . . ." "Yes, March. To

par•a•phrase the proverb: a guest, like fish, begins to stink after three days. Unless there's a Miss Carter who's been sprinkling cologne. Arrest them, Inspector!"

Brazzaville — breathy

"So, what's an Ivy League type like you doing in

Braz•za•ville , pal? Get separated from your Boy Scout troop? The Congo's no place for an innocent from Columbia." Through a

breach in the drape, Harmon could see that the listless dancing in the other room had stopped. So, too, had the tinny noise of the juke box, stocked with ancient 45s. "It was

breach of promise ," Flood replied after a while. He didn't even look up at Harmon but continued to move the playing cards around. Harmon laughed. "Well, sonny, my style has usually been

breach of the peace . So let's hear it. You duck out on a babe and her angry pop?" Flood turned over another card on the sticky plastic tablecloth. "Something like that. Call it

breach of trust , then. I didn't like what I did. Wish I could do it over." "So what do you do for

bread , man? Your suit doesn't look too clean. You must be hard up by now." "Yeah." "Well, my

bread-and-but•ter is . . . transportation, shall we say. I could throw a job your way. Interested?" Harmon patted his own

bread•bas•ket　　and laughed again. "But you gotta have the stomach for it. No Ivy League prissiness, O.K.?" In response, Flood yanked the knife from the moldy loaf on the

bread•board　　and waved it just below Harmon's bulging eyes. "Enough with the Ivy League crap. What the hell would I be transporting?" Harmon caught his breath. "Let's just say it's no bigger than a

bread•box　　. A small piece of machinery that can help make things go boom— after flying far above these damn shrubs and

bread•fruit　　trees. And I think that's all you need to know." "Yeah? So I risk my life, and you tell me practically squat?" Harmon laughed again. "My boy, think of the

bread line　　you'd be on without me. You wouldn't want that, would you?" He sawed off another piece from the loaf and brought it to his lips,

bread mold　　and all. Flood said nothing, but he was thinking of the vast prairies of his home state, the cooling breeze at evening, the

bread•root　　and the wind-swept grass. And Sally's freckled hand, dipping into the sack of

bread•stuff　　as she prepared to make his favorite loaf: rye. But at least he appeared to have made contact with Code Name A. The next day, Flood sat glumly comparing the

breadth	of the truck he had been driving and the width of the lane between the security booths. No question:
breadth•ways	it would be tight. But there was no choice. Somehow, they were on the alert. Had someone passed the word? "You're the
bread•win•ner	now, boy! Let's see what this baby can do!" With a roar, the truck picked up the speed needed to
break	through the barrier. Suddenly, an armed policeman leaped into the lane. "Tough
break	, sergeant. It's you or me!" For a moment, the man held his ground. Then, shrieking, he dived out of the way. Smash! Everything
break•a•ble	was shattered; pieces of wood, straw, and brick littered the rutted road. Shots rang out. Flood surveyed the
break•age	in the rear-view mirror. The package was still on the seat beside him. "Time for our
break•a•way	," he said, pushing the accelerator to the floor. The truck went tearing through a giant pothole, rattling his limbs like
break•bone fever	. Then, some miles later, he saw the fuel gauge fluttering. "Oh, God, it's not the time for a
break•down	!" Or had a bullet hit something? Just then, a half dozen logs came spilling out

of the jungle onto the dirt road. The truck went flying like a white-capped

break•er

at Jones Beach and landed crazily on two wheels. More logs! Someone certainly had expected him. The steering wheel jerked. "Breaker,

break•er

!" he shouted into the CB. The jungle trees ran up to meet him. And then everything went black. . . .
"Do you prefer coffee with

break•fast

? Or tea?" Flood murmured. Then, eyes wide in surprise, he saw her. Using his Columbia vocabulary, he thought: a real stunner! "You Americans often like prepackaged

breakfast food

, don't you? Cold cereal?" "Where am I?" Flood bolted to the window and peered outside: sheer walls, topped with barbed wire. And at the

break•front

was a mounted machinegun. "How did I get here?" *It must be B.* The blonde laughed. "You can call me Olga. And it was a case of

breaking and entering

, shall we say? Your truck came into our lives — rather uninvited." Flood's head pounded, and he flinched. "Oh, I hope you haven't reached your

breaking point

yet. You've still got a long way to go." "Where's my truck?" She smiled grimly. "At that

31

break•neck	speed? I'm afraid it didn't survive. Now, Mr. Flood — yes, we know who you are — you will perform a heroic
break•out	from our camp and continue on the mission entrusted to you by Harmon. Your help could give us the
break•through	we need to destroy his operation." "And what operation is that?" asked Flood, sampling the toast. "Ever since the
break•up	of the military junta, arms dealers have squared off. Simply put, we are rivals of Harmon. Listen carefully if you want to save your life." 　　　　　Scanning the area beyond the
break•wa•ter	with the binoculars, Flood watched the men on the ship eating a simple meal. A bearded sailor swallowed a pair of
bream	, then followed it with a long draught of wine. Another man, on his knees, tried to
bream	the deck where an unpleasant spill had stained the wood. Meanwhile, close behind Flood was Olga, her
breast	pressed against his back. Under different circumstances, it might have been pleasant, but he knew that taped just below her
breast•bone	was plastic explosive — enough to wreak havoc on Harmon's ship. "Now remember: I am anthropologist Martha

Breas•ted	, and I was in the jungle, about to
breast-feed	my baby when she was kidnapped. You've agreed to help get her back. That should make me seem pretty harmless. O.K.?" "Yeah." Flood dared a look at his Columbia
breast•pin	, then climbed to his feet. "You sure that explosive is safe? I'd feel better if you had a
breast•plate	or something." "That would show. Come on. They're expecting their package." Just then, one of the sailors gave a shout: A swimmer doing a somewhat clumsy version of the
breast stroke	was drawing near the ship. The men on deck greeted him raucously. "Do you recognize him?" "No. Let's see if we can reach the
breast•work	before they fill us with bullets." "That's encouraging," muttered Flood, taking a deep
breath	. This was insane! He'd probably flunk a
Breath•a•lyz•er	test right now, the way his pulse was racing and his thoughts going haywire. As they walked, he could hardly
breathe	. Martha seemed cool, even though she knew the ship was loaded withmunitions. At the ramp, up to, a foul-

breathed	sailor came face to face with them and motioned with his Uzi. "Bring them on board," came a voice. Then: "Well, well! It's Mr. Flood! Why don't you take a
breath•er	while we deal with your new friend." Harmon stepped out of the shadow of the cabin. "We've been expecting you." Harmon's
breath•ing	came loudly. Had he been the swimmer? Flood had no time to ponder, because he sensed that his companion was about to tear off the explosive. No
breathing space	at all! Hurling himself over the side of the ship, Flood dropped like a dead weight into the murky water. He was nearly
breath•less	when, half a minute later, he broke the surface again. Gulping air, he looked around him. The ship was a
breath•tak•ing	pyre, and rockets were streaking in all directions, like a fireworks display gone mad. He straggled to shore, just as a
breath•y	voice issued from his breastpin: "From the sounds of things, Mr. Flood, you've achieved your mission. A and B destroyed. Helicopter on its way."

34

xerosis — X.i.

"The worst sin of all is the sin of pride,
especially the pride of believing you
are without sin. The self-deluded person
is like the man with

xe•ro•sis

, who feels that patch of skin growing
drier and drier and then spreading – but
how he denies it! How he keeps it under
his sleeve, out of sight. But men and
women are not

xe•ro•ther•mic

. They can't live in such abnormally dry
circumstances. Only the soothing
touch of Our Lord will cure that condition. You can have all the shares you
want of Exxon Mobil or SterlingCorp or

Xe•rox

, but you will never gain the Kingdom of
Heaven without admitting your sin. You
can wield the power of Nebuchadnezzar or

Xerx•es I

, but your strength will be as a broken
reed in the face of Our Savior's fierce
wind, which will blow from the arctic
wastes to the torrid land of the

Xho•sa

. You may pride yourself on your learning,
able to solve perplexing mathematical
problems. You may master Greek,
knowing your pi from your

xi

– but what truly counts is He Who is
Alpha and Omega. He is Wise beyond
wisdom, All-Knowing beyond knowledge.
He is the Prime Dictionary. He is the

X.i. and learn to make it grow a hundred-fold." He studied himself in the mirror. "Not bad," he said. "Now go knock 'em dead."

erlking —— erogenous

What is not known by the casual readers of Hudson's Victorian fairy tales is his interest in probing the limits of propriety. In his tale about the

erl•king

in the garden, which his publisher refused to include in the '83 edition, the spirit appears in a tree overhanging the fountain (representing amoral nature, presumably), dressed in white

er•mine

and sporting a feathered cap. The two children of the wealthy banker, here a bit older than most of Hudson's young characters, spot this

er•mined

imp making faces at himself in the fountain's rippling water. "Come down from there and tell us who you are," shouts Percy. All at once, a magnificent

erne

appears overhead, winging to the sea, and when the children look back to the tree, the mysterious visitor is beside them. "Oh, you must be

Er•nest

, the cook's nephew!" exclaims Edwina, as he gives her a kiss. "You mustn't do that!" But when the visitor does the same with Percy, the lad exclaims, "It must be

Er•nes•tine

, rather, with those soft lips!" Then, as the children flee and the visitor chases them through the garden maze, a scene like something out of Max

Ernst   's surrealistic collages occurs: berries giggle, grass purrs. The reality — and the morality — that held Percy and Edwina in place begins to

e•rode   . And although Hudson's prose becomes deliberately opaque and allusive, it is clear that each child discovers an unsuspected

e•rog•e•nous   hideaway in the garden, where they are visited by this subversive spirit. No surprise, too, that their mother (symbol of order) comes to a bad end.

homestretch — homing pigeon

She told herself that the

home•stretch   was coming. If she could get to it, and then get past it, she would be all right. It would be over when she was in the car again, heading

home•ward   . Then she'd try to let it all slip away. Let the familiar take over, not this terrible newness. The familiar would help. It would save her. But the table in the kitchen where he used to do his

home•work   would be there. Too familiar. The bedroom upstairs. She would not go there. Would the place ever feel

hom•ey   again? How could it? How could it, tell me that. It's not that she felt a

hom•i•ci•dal   rage, because that would change nothing. It would not bring him back. He would never be back. And wasn't one death just like another, when the result was the same, car accident or

hom•i•cide   or the stealthy, devilishly efficient thing that took over his body and took him away. How many times already had she heard a

hom•i•let•ic   comment from a friend or a neighbor? They could not say anything else. What else was there to say? God has a plan. It was totally random. There is a reason.

39

And now, a true student of

hom•i•let•ics , in the person of Father McGuire.
Grave, dignified, forceful of expression
– all the things that her son had not been
in the last days. His voice had been
barely a whisper. . . . And the

hom•i•list was saying something, she didn't catch
it. There were people on either side of
her, sitting with straight backs in the
pew. And soon, before she knew it, the

hom•i•ly was in full swing. The homestretch? Or
would that be at the grave? As long as
Father didn't mention his name more
than four or five times. Two times. The
soul, if it exists, does it go

hom•ing , searching for a preordained destination?
A dove, a snow-white hawk, a

homing pigeon , rising translucently toward something.
Searching. She looked into the bleeding
colors of the stained-glass windows.
Grasped the firm wood of the pew.
Waited for her gaping wound to close.

infinitude — inflation

Q. awakes this particular morning and, heedless, gets up on the wrong side of the bed. He stumbles toward the bathroom, which seems to take an

in•fin•i•tude   . At last, feeling 30 years older, he reaches it and stares into the mirror. An

in•fin•i•ty   of mirrors returns his perplexed scowl. He spins around to flee, but all at once he feels

in•firm   , scarcely able to move faster than a snail. "Good morning, Father," says his son. "Let us go to the

in•fir•ma•ry   ; you look so weak and tired." "No, no, my only

in•fir•mi•ty   is doubt. This cannot be!" The son laughs. "Come, Father. The good doctor can

in•fix   you with the proper vitamins to restore you." So Q. finds himself waiting in the infirmary. A door is ajar. Q. crawls toward it. Beyond,

in fla•gran•te de•lic•to   , a naked couple moans and grapples. The sight is about to

in•flame   Q.'s senses when he perceives it is his wife — and the doctor. Q. gasps. Then the doctor, dressed, tells him severely that the human spirit is

in•flam•ma•ble , dangerously so. "Look here," he says, finger poking Q.'s ribs. "Clearly an

in•flam•ma•tion of the heart, quite near to breaking through the skin." "Are you certain?" asks Q., collapsing in the chair. "Oh, yes. You must stop this

in•flam•ma•to•ry behavior, or you'll not last long. You must give your vacuoles a little rest. I can tell you your good wife is very concerned." "Where is she?" asks Q., watching the doctor

in•flate the pressure cuff of the sphygmoma-nometer around his arm. "Where is who?" "My wife." "Your wife is perfectly healthy," he replies. The band is now

in•flat•ed , and Q. feels a disquieting constriction, spreading from his arm. "Why on earth should she be here?" The doctor frowns paternally. "I don't want to risk a perilous

in•fla•tion of hope, my dear sir, but go home, go to bed, shake hands with your lovely wife — and tomorrow make sure to get up on the right side of the bed."

Hancock —— handicap

The pompous imbecile in the uniform, all badges and gold braid, stares at my passport. In his thick Middle Eastern accent, he repeats my name. Of course, my John

Han•cock is not genuine. Glances at me again. Then, grudgingly, waves his

hand and I pass. "Thank God," I say to myself. But it's certainly not the typical American god I invoke, a plump bearded fellow who beams down on his smug congregation as the members walk

hand- in-hand to their comfortable pews. No, my God has nothing to do with false sentimentality. My God is probably more like that official's, a God who raises his mighty

Hand of Wrath, bringing righteous havoc to the godless masses. And to their rulers. In His Name I am honored to wield my own smaller

hand ax whenever I can. Now what? Another functionary hurries toward me. I could silence him with a blow to the windpipe. He gestures. "Your

hand•bag , please. It has been checked?" How do you think I got through security, idiot? His supercilious stare reminds me of a former professor of mine who prided himself as a cerebral

hand•ball player. Loved to reminisce about his victories, loved to use the infantile game as a metaphor for whatever outdated philosophical theory he was expounding. He can go to hell in a

hand•bar•row or whatever the metaphor is. Still, I admit that stealth and misdirection can be useful. The security person probes my bag. Good thing I had tossed the

hand•bill demanding the immediate ouster and prosecution of the nation's president. I know where I can get more copies. Mr. Officious waves me on. I pass a ridiculous

hand•blown glass statuette, symbolizing Liberty or Democracy or Satiety or some such idol of our modern age. This land makes even less pretense to live up those fantasies than most. The stolen

hand•book , taken from a rather careless C.I.A. operative, made that clear, despite the American rhetoric of "time-tested bonds and a dedication to human dignity." Sure. Apparently there's a

hand•breadth between championing human dignity and stringing dissenters up by their feet in the public square and gouging out their eyes. What advances have the ties with the U.S. brought? Using a

hand•car	instead of a camel or bicycle to get from one prison to another, as in some ridiculous silent film? And it's hard to push a
hand•cart	in the pretty new supermarkets when your hands have been cut off for bad-mouthing the dictator. Excuse me, the president. Or, to be more accurate, president-for-life. Yes, that historic
hand•clasp	between America's empty-headed ambassador and the president, captured forever in photos. Nice fat bribe in the president's pocket. Corruption here is an art, more practiced than any
hand•craft	or public service. As I walk outside, the air is hot and even grainy on my forehead. Ah, a first glimpse of the police at work, snapping closed a
hand•cuff	on the slender wrist of a hungry-looking youth. Did he fail to sing the praise of the rulers? Unless he begs for mercy and spills some names, will he be
hand•ed	over to those expert practitioners in the prison's cellars? This had long been a culture of
hand•ed•ness	, where one hand is used to eat with, the other to wipe your ass with – and never the twain shall meet. Which does the interrogator use as he . . . extracts a confession? Perhaps he listens to
Han•del	as he works, like those cultured Nazis. Or Beethoven. No, probably a more

local musician. This ruling tribe, or junta, or party – bound together by a sacred

hand•fast   in its early years. Now the pretense is mostly gone. No better in my own progressive nation, where hypocrisy rules. There's comfort only if you look a certain way and have money. The only

hand•fast•ing   you'd see in this land today is when these pigs loot the public treasury as fast as they can, hand over fist. And their leader, always ready for good p.r., loves to

hand-feed   a sprightly little girl as she sits on his starched uniform trousers and the cameras flash and whir. And the world goes "ooooh!" Then the president-for-life tosses a

hand•ful   of coins into a group of urchins – who no doubt were given clean clothes for the scene – and laughs beneficently as they scramble for them. Off camera, he examines himself in a

hand glass   held at face level by one of his aides. Yes, paternal. Yes, magnanimous. Well, back to the looting. I would love to stuff a

hand grenade   into his mouth and pull the pin. . . . Oh, he'll be shocked when the global conference this sham democracy is hosting becomes a hellhole. That I can guarantee. With God's help, that is. The

hand•grip   on my travel bag is already moist with sweat. Where is the damn hotel? Then,

46

after a brief meal, off to see my contact,
who has guaranteed at least a

hand•gun

for my use. The explosives should also
be in the arranged place. My last visit, I
was able to inch myself up the wall in
question with a cleverly concealed

hand•hold

or two. Then to pick up the wheelchair
and stuff it with the explosives. At the
conference, they'll rush to make a path
for me, so moved by my

hand•i•cap

and my brave efforts. Get as close to the
stage – and the big shots – as possible.
Human dregs all. And then . . . a memo-
rable farewell to this fallen world.

journey — jovial

"Life, Billy Joe, is like a

jour•ney   between where you come from and
where you wanna go. We may not like
it, but it's God's plan for us. We all have
to make that journey. Every one of us —
even me — is only a

jour•ney•man   travelin' between those points, doing
what we can, doing what needs to be
done. Sometimes, with hard work and
dedication, we succeed. Sometimes, it's
just

jour•ney•work   ; nothin' to write home about, you
understand, but we can still be proud
'cause we tried. But sometimes, we stink
up the place — because we don't have
our heads screwed on right. So, as we

joust   against the demonic forces out there
against us on the great field of life, Billy
Joe, I want you to stare them down, by

Jove   , and give it your best shot, all you've
got. You know me — I like to kick back,
take it easy, and be the

jo•vi•al   sort. But I gotta tell you, son, if you
keep throwin' those damn interceptions,
I'll haul your ass clear outta there!"

mostly — mother

Sure, I'll admit it: My clients are scum,

most•ly . But if they can pay. . . . So when Bennie the Bloodsucker waved a round-trip ticket to

Mo•sul and told me to "drop off" something with Nasif and "pick up" something else, I was on my way pretty damn quick. Sure, our password wasn't exactly a

mot , but we can't all be Simon Templar, right? "The kings of Nineveh are now dust in the wind." Said my contact: "Yet the Tigris rolls on." Exchanged the packages, but then I got a

mote in one of the old peepers. The damn desert sand, I suppose. Couldn't see too well, and in *my* business. . . . "Pardon, monsieur, have you a little

mote bothering your eye?" she asked, entering my life with all the subtlety of a land slide. Curves, lips, eyelashes. Sure, I'm fast. We were in the only decent

mo•tel in the damn city fifteen minutes later, and with the right coaxing Soraya was singing up a storm, and I don't mean some goddamn medieval

mo•tet , while showing me some pretty good moves. Yeah, so maybe she was the flame, and I was the

49

moth , the fall guy. But she wasn't quite good enough, 'cause when the shooting started, I hit the deck. Like I say, I'm fast. Poor Soraya! Holes big enough to toss a

moth•ball through. But I'm out over the terrace. Nasif is cursing, and I'm running for my life, my

moth-eaten raincoat flapping in the gritty breeze. The package? I figure maybe it's Bennie's — or maybe my dear

moth•er would dig a nice little present. At least she never set me up for a measly ten grand.

offend — office boy

Part I
DAVE: Don't mean to

of•fend

your delicate sensibilities, Ron, but your
favorites are stinking up the joint. The
defense is moving at half-speed, the

of•fense

has about as much bite as a hamster, and
the special teams seem afraid to tackle
the guy with the ball. RON: Look, my
friend, when it comes to running an

of•fense•less

offense, we don't have to look far. In
your old scheme, the wide receivers
were only decoys, so the coach could
have the running back slam into the line
for no gain – time after time! To me, *that's*

of•fen•sive

! TROY: But let's not forget the front office that put this bunch of losers on the
field with only the vaguest notion of
what they should be doing! There's just
no strategy! I'm tempted to

of•fer

my services – and I've been out of the
game for eight years now. DAVE: The
game has passed you by, Troy, old pal,
but thanks for

of•fer•ing

. And this particular coach ain't gonna
take any suggestions from anyone!
That's part of the problem. Last season,
we had a group of analysts put together
a super-fine

of•fer•to•ry   of a complete game plan, with all the x's and o's you could ever want, and he just did a quick

off-glide   and slipped back into his den. RON: Look, Mr. Know-It-All, that's because you genius boys made a big production of it! Coach isn't going to take that! No, you need to give advice

off•hand   , like you just thought of it. That way, he can nod and mumble something about considering it down the road and then go think it over in his

of•fice   , away from all you loud-mouthed critics! TROY: But down the road is now, baby! He's just about out of time to turn this team around. Even some snot-nosed

office boy   can tell that they need a strategy that takes advantage of the other team's weaknesses – and they've gotta disguise their plays better. Am I right or am I right?

Part II
DAVID: There are so many things wrong with your interpretation, Ronald, that I don't know where to start. I don't mean to

of•fend   you and your party of spineless accommodators, but if the president did what you suggest, our nation would lack a flexible force of sufficient

of•fense   to make retaliation credible. As simple as that. RONALD: Everything is as simple as that for you people . . . and that's why we're in this mess to begin with. Our troops are

of•fense•less

as it is, because of the secretary's pipe dream about a lighter, swifter ground force. That didn't work, and it would never work in today's world. TROY: But the most recent

of•fen•sive

into the insurgent-controlled territory showed promise. We just have to let the generals there make the decisions, not some inexperienced hothead at a desk in D.C. RONALD: I'll

of•fer

this opinion: Don't forget that this administration sent an ill-equipped army over there with only the vaguest notion of what it should be doing! There's just no strategy! But if anyone's

of•fer•ing

counsel, you can be sure that the admin-istration won't even pretend to listen. They're an insular bunch, guided solely by ideology. TROY: They expect us to genuflect at their

of•fer•to•ry

service without making sure of what's actually being offered! Or, to change the metaphor, it's all

off-glide

and silence – nothing we can really evaluate. DAVID: While my colleague takes a few deep breaths and remembers that he's no longer the Smartest Boy at Yale, let me say that the secretary's

off•hand   comment about going to war with the army you have was merely a realistic assessment, given our multiple responsibilities around the world. RONALD: But the president still insulates himself in his

of•fice   , reading only pre-selected reports. Even if he opens his eyes, is there time to turn this war around? TROY: Not if he continues to treat his most sensible advisor like an

office boy   ! I think all three of us can agree on that score.

Chablis — chador

"Wine can make me do the strangest things, my dear, like the time all that

Cha•blis

went straight to my head, and I did a stunning little

cha-cha

with that adorable pet of Billy's. Billy, what's that animal of yours? A gibbon?" "Oh, how plebeian, Jackie. Mine's a

chac•ma

, the only one on this coast." "Well, then I must beg your pardon, dearest. Aren't *we* touchy! But anyway, in

Cha•co

once, at Jake and Muffy's — what bores *they've* become, Billy, hard to believe — Stan and I composed a

cha•conne

for harpsichord and kazoo, and neither of us could play at all! Muffy simply loved it." "Of course it's

cha•cun à son goût

, though God knows they've no *goût* to speak of." "Don't listen to Billy. And he's no one to talk. That time we went to the film festival near Lake

Chad

, you know, he got roaring drunk and chased all the native girls, just begging for a little peek under the caftan or yashmak or

cha•dor

or whatever those dumpy robes are called."

"I suppose you know, Professor Silver, that you've always been a hero to me, a model to follow." Brown shifted the thermos containing the

i•ci•cle   from one hand to the other and leaned back in his chair. Across his large, defiantly old-fashioned desk, its surface almost entirely covered by neat piles of paper, Silver looked back at him

i•ci•ly   . Behind the desk was a tall screen on which he had pinned some images – both holy figures and movie stars. Brown had interrupted his terribly important work, thus the attitude of

i•ci•ness   . Very well, thought Brown. Harden my heart and make my task easier. Seeing his expression will be

ic•ing   on the cake. The electric fireplace – no doubt Silver disliked such modernity in the venerable college – was quietly at work. Inside Brown's jacket was his passport. Where he planned to go, the

ICJ   had no jurisdiction, and the police would never find him. That would show them all that he was not, as the damn departmental review put it, "sorely lacking in industry and insight." It would be

ick•y   seeing old Silver's blood on the desk and on the pages and pages of scholarly work. Ancient history – which is what Silver will be when I'm done. "You might even say you've been an

i•con to me. Ironic, isn't it, given one of your principal areas of study." Silver's expression did not change. "There's such a cheapening of language these days," he said. "Today the noble word

i•con•ic has lost almost all meaning when every Tom, Dick, and Britney is labeled as such." Brown shifted uneasily in his chair, still clasping the thermos. "Professor Silver, have you ever visited

I•co•ni•um ? That would seem fitting." "The ancient name of Konya, in what is now Turkey. One would be unlikely to find icons there under the rule of the Seljuk Turks or the Ottomans. The combinational form

i•con•o- was originally spelled eikono, Professor Brown. So the resemblance is shallow." Silver seemed to be staring at the thermos. Brown shifted it to the other hand again. "Isn't some active

i•con•o•clasm a necessary part of the Hegelian dialectic, Professor Silver?" The revered scholar gave a dismissive sniff. "Like most of you younger folk, Professor Brown, you likely conceive of yourself as an

i•con•o•clast , shattering outdated ways of thinking – and perhaps some outdated people along the way." Brown shivered. "As a lover of history and art, I firmly believe that a life spent on such fields as

i•co•nog•ra•phy is valuable," continued the older man, glancing at his neat piles of papers. "Oh, no doubt," replied Brown quickly. "But when it degenerates into

i•co•nol•a•try , that is an entirely different matter. Then it becomes time to clear the terrain." He glanced over his shoulder to make sure the office door was closed. "There is," said Silver dryly, "some fascinating

i•co•nol•o•gy about that brave young woman, Jael, killing the Canaanite commander Sisera with a tent pin. The study of icons and illustrative images and symbols tells us much. Oh, I should add that an

i•con•o•scope or some such modern device is filming this meeting. Damn it, man! Did you really think you're the first colleague or graduate student who's tried to murder me?" Brown gaped. "Behind that

i•co•nos•ta•sis – or screen, if you prefer – waits one of the university policemen. I presume you have an icicle in your thermos? You'd stab me, then destroy the evidence in the fireplace. Your plot wasn't a complex

i•co•sa•he•dron , dear boy. It was plain as day – and pla-giarized! I read that story eons ago, when I had time for such nonsense." As the officer emerged from behind the screen, he added. "See you at the trial."

swashbuckler — swath

"Oh, I'm afraid my days as a

swash•buck•ler

are long past!" he said with a quiet chuckle. "We'll leave that sort of thing to all you younger folks starting out in government service." He nodded toward the questioner. "Yes,

swash•buck•ling

is definitely for the young." As he paused to take a sip from his plain brown mug, there was a muffled yell from the back of the auditorium, and a sudden

swash•ing

down the main aisle. A young man came running toward the stage with a placard, its carefully drawn

swash letters

denouncing the great man in somewhat vulgar terms. "Oh, a

swas•ti•ka

as well, I see," said the guest from his comfortable chair on the stage. "As un-imaginative as ever!" The security people were advancing on the intruder. "I believe it was the princely state of

Swat

in old India that used such a figure centuries before Adolf spoiled it for all of us." He gave another dry chuckle. "We can all learn from history." "I'd like to

swat

you, you butcher! You send our soldiers off to die in a foreign land – but how many draft exemptions did you have? Five?" Just before the first security officer grabbed him, he flung a

swatch onto the stage. Loud gasps. "Not to worry, please," said the guest. "It's more symbolism. Blood on a G.I.'s shirt, no doubt. Again, how unoriginal!" Appreciative laughter. Four suited men made a

swath through the audience as they led the protestor away. "Now, I believe I have time for one or two more questions."

respiratory system — resuscitator

respiratory system

re•spire

res•pite

re•splend•ent

re•spond

re•spond•ent

re•spond•er

"I should have taken better care of myself." After drink and drugs and various forms of excess – some better left in memory's shadows – his hands occasionally shook and his

was . . . well, let's just say it was not always reliable. As long as Maxwell could

most of the time, he'd be all right. But tonight, with a gibbous moon and a breeze that carried the noxious perfume of a charnel house, he tossed the spade aside and took a brief

. He had counted on the moon's being more

than it was this night, because he could not risk bringing a lantern. He could not let anyone find him here, in this grave-yard. How could he

if the thick-headed village constable was called by some busybody? "And just what do you think you're doing, Mr. American?" Next thing you know, he'd be hauled up as a

at some ridiculous inquest. And the moment would be lost – possibly forever. He had begun the mystic call. Now he had to see if there would be a

. A nice euphemism there! Maxwell

wiped the sweat from his brow, peered behind him toward the cemetery's gate. Too dark to see its rusty bars. He laughed. What sort of horrible

re•sponse would come from the being he'd summoned? Not a nice one, not nice at all, and it would be up to him to keep things manageable. And despite his shaky hands, he felt he could bear the

re•spon•si•bil•i•ty . And if not, it wouldn't matter! Because it would all be over: his life, the whole race of puny humans, this planet as we knew it. And in some ways, Piggott – rotting in his grave – would be just as

re•spon•si•ble , for it was his cryptic writing that had led Maxwell to this point. If Maxwell hadn't discovered the manuscript of Piggott's vile Oxford

re•spon•sion , when the budding scholar, possibly already out of his mind, had scrawled instructions for the Summoning and shocked the dry dons who had expected the same old rehashing! Oh, they were

re•spon•sive , that was plain: they'd had young Piggott hauled away to the nearest prison for the dangerously insane. But being clerics, no doubt they'd also intoned some sort of

re•spon•so•ry for the good of his eternal soul. And 200 years later, it was Maxwell's awesome opportunity to follow through on Piggott's vile hints. How ironic that the welfare of the

res publica	was now in Maxwell's hands! He coughed, looking around again. The breeze whispered darkly. In his pocket was his copy of Piggott's words. When the time was right . . . but he did need to
rest	. He was not a young man. Still, he was not in the least like those desiccated Oxford dons who had looked down at him when he arrived from the States, with his antiquarian queries. And the
rest	of them, the doubters, those who had scorned him! They would learn. Especially Silas Trump, self-professed antiquarian. "Let me see if I can
re•state	your claims, Maxwell." They were in a small
res•tau•rant	in Arkham – hell, it was a greasy spoon, that's what it was – huddled in one of the booths farthest from the windows. "You're telling me that loony Piggott was . . ." He fell silent as the
res•tau•ra•teur	, a slovenly type who was never seen without his apron, passed too close to the table. "So Piggott managed to translate some phrases in the *Necronomicon* from Arabic into English? You need a
rest cure	, my friend. How would Piggott know Arabic? And why wouldn't his tutors or whatever they're called at Oxford have confiscated his ravings?" Maxwell tried his best to maintain his

rest•ful	demeanor, but it was difficult. The man obviously had a skull full of
rest•har•row	and dandelions, not brains! As Trump prattled on, Maxwell tried to imagine how the pompous ass would shriek in the many oozing
res•ti•form	limbs of Yog-Sothoth. If that indeed was his incarnation. Well, if Trump was not interested in helping to rouse the
rest•ing	god, then he'd not share in the glory. He'd cheated Maxwell once or twice in the past, gotten hold of invaluable charms and blocked his path to knowledge. Trump would make
res•ti•tu•tion	, no doubt about that . . . before feeding the hungry lord. But even as Trump recited all the reasons the trip to England was foolish, he seemed
res•tive	, fidgety, as if something troubled him. He nearly knocked over his beer as he sweepingly dismissed the whole plan. "Fine, bow out, Trump. I don't need you. And you're acting tense and
rest•less	, anyway. Wouldn't be much help." "What are you talking about! I'm not tense!" "Hell, man, you're acting like a
restless cavy	who's just blundered into a den of jaguars!" Trump shook his head. "It's just a few . . . business concerns. I'm extended a bit too much." "Do what I do to take my mind off things. Ponder

rest mass or the concept of an entire novel without the letter 'e' or Abelian groups or . . ." "Very helpful," snapped Trump, rising. "Have fun on your vacation." Not quite, Maxwell thought. More a

res•tor•a•tion , in which his proper place in the universe would be made clear to everyone. But enough dawdling. He'd had his

res•tor•a•tive daydreaming. Back to the reality of hard earth, sickly breeze, chilly night. But as he picked up the spade again, he wished some unbeliever like Trump could witness his work to

re•store the true state of existence. Translating Abdul Alhazred's feverish poetry, Piggott had scrawled in the margins of his Oxford examination what looked like

restr. – meaning what? Restaurant? Unlikely. It was even unclear whether it was Latin – in which he'd written his answers – or the English he'd lapsed into for his ravings. Perhaps

re•strain or restriction? Maxwell could certainly imagine needing some kind of powerful supernatural amulet or

re•strain•er once the god had answered his summons. It's not as if you could wave a

restraining order in his its? – face! If there was a face, that is, and not just a gelatinous hulk with a maw of a thousand razor-sharp teeth. Maxwell resumed digging without

re•straint	, feeling new urgency. And it was only minutes later that he felt the spade hit something harder than earth. He dropped to his knees and began to scrape away the dirt. Wood. There'd be no
restraint of trade	, nothing to stand in his way now! With the handle of the spade, he smashed through the ancient coffin. Then he thrust his hand into the darkness. Nothing to
re•strict	his movements until he felt a small, cold, hard thing. A finger – Piggott's! Or should he say finger bones? Controlling his repulsion, he felt around. Something harder. His breath came as if
re•strict•ed	. With an exclamation that was part curse, part prayer, he pulled it off Piggott's dead finger. And slipped it onto his own, half convinced that it would vanish nonetheless. "There's a
re•stric•tion	against grave-robbers, Maxwell." As the cold snaked down his spine, Maxwell looked up from the hole he was standing in. "There's a very persuasive reason for such
re•stric•tion•ism	– respect for private property, respect for the unearthly forces that somehow seem to collect around places like this." "You talk too much, Trump," he responded. "Ah. No, I'm afraid we must be
re•stric•tive	at this point," said Trump as Maxwell tried to scramble out of the grave. "My colleagues here" – Trump gestured, his

restrictive covenant

rest room

re•struc•ture

re•sult

re•sult•ant

re•sume

ré•su•mé

face partly visible in the moonlight – "will make sure of that. A kind of

." "As I said, you talk too damn much," snapped Maxwell. "But don't think you're getting Piggott's invocation. That is, unless you come down here to join me." "Smells a bit like an untended

, so I'll decline. Hand it up, or Trevor and Nigel will be forced to take it from you." Maxwell said nothing. "Think, my friend. I wouldn't want them to

your face for you." As if they would let him walk away even if he gave them what they wanted. Finally, with an exag-gerated sigh, he reached into his pocket. The immediate

was the loud – uncannily loud – cocking of pistols. "I don't have a gun, you moron. What use would a gun be with . . The Guardian of the Gate?" "True," said Trump. "The

melee would not be pretty. The paper." Maxwell dug out the paper he had brought with him and held it up. "Thank you," said Trump, snatching it. "You can

your digging. It's Piggott's grave, I gather. What I don't understand is why, with a sterling

in the dark arts like his, he achieved nothing. If he could indeed summon Yog-Sothoth from his extra-dimensional home, why did he end so badly, with so little to show?" Maxwell halted his

re•sump•tion of the digging, trying to make out the brutish faces of the two local thugs Trump had hired. "A failure of nerve, perhaps." "You seem nervous, too. To take your mind off things, consider the

re•su•pi•nate orchid or recall Abélard's *Sic et Non*, or think of those quiet days of your youth – you were young once, weren't you? – when you lazed along the Miskatonic River,

re•su•pine , letting the sunlight tickle your eyelids." "Very poetic, Trump. But none of it will help my nerves if the god does

re•sur•face , if you're foolish enough to utter the incantation." Trump laughed. "Shall we try? 'Arise, awaken, appear, O Mighty One, both Gate and Guardian of the Gate! Arise and

re•surge from Your troubled sleep! This I bid You, O Yog-Sothoth!' And let me add, Maxwell, if these words from Piggott fail to work, you will . . ." Suddenly, the heaped soil from the grave seemed to be

re•sur•gent , animated, mindful. It swirled off the ground, glowing with a frightening colorless light. Then its shape changed – and swelled. "With these words," shouted Trump deliriously, "I Thee

res•ur•rect !" The sky crackled. Overhead, the shape grew and grew. Maxwell glimpsed a vast globular thing before squeezing his eyes shut. He stroked the skeleton's ring, reciting its charm as the

res•ur•rec•tion

continued. He heard Trump gasp, he heard the two thugs howl in fear . . . and then agony. "My God, Maxwell, it's –" But the words were snuffed. So Trump had learned the hard way that

res•ur•rec•tion•ism

was not a fool's game. To be safe, Maxwell recited the charm again. Then, all at once, there was silence. When he opened his eyes, he saw only the moon smudged by clouds. The would-be

res•ur•rec•tion•ist

and his local thugs lay dead. No sign of Yog-Sothoth, except for the gouged land, the shriveled grass, the scent of burning. The only thing that would ever grow here again was a

resurrection plant

, thought Maxwell. But Yog-Sothoth was the god of resurrection, and Maxwell had memorized Piggott's incantations. "Lord Yog-Sothoth, I beg You,

re•sus•ci•tate

these creatures, in Your honor." A moment later, Trump's eyes blinked. He breathed hoarsely. Sounds worse than me, thought Maxwell with a laugh, thanking the dread

re•sus•ci•ta•tor

. Restr.? The two thugs stood by, expressionless. Trump gazed blankly at him, waiting. "Well," said Maxwell, "you wouldn't work with me alive – but you'll damn well work for me dead."

dominance — Dominic

It's all about

dom·i·nance , no question about that. You confront a challenge, you sneer in the face of the competitor, you seek to crush his spirit until he, too, recognizes that you are the

dom·i·nant one, that he is as nothing to you. And you must

dom·i·nate , because that is your reason for being. Some people are born for subjugation, others for

dom·i·na·tion , and the true winners know who they are. Clausewitz says it is not enough to achieve victory – no, you must

dom·i·neer . And Sun Tzu says much the same thing, noting in his famous thirteenth chapter that the losers only truly recognize their superiors when they are

dom·i·neer·ing , as simple as that. So . . . it is time to face another challenger and add another fabulous chapter to my immortal legacy. Years from now, when — "Damn it,

Dom·i·nic , how many times do I have to call? Stop with the thumb wrestling, come inside, and wash your hands for dinner!"

Eckhart — ecstatic

Eck·hart

é·clair

é·clair·cisse·ment

ec·lamp·si·a

é·clat

ec·lec·tic

"You know, when Gary gets on a roll and starts spewing that business-school jargon, I sometimes feel like I've wandered into a sermon by Meister

and I don't have a clue what's going on!" "Tell me about it," replied Shaw, wondering who the hell Eckhart was. There was a lot he didn't know. "Want the last

?" he asked Bozzone. "That's actually a cannoli, bud. You don't know the difference?" "Well, my family didn't go in much for fancy desserts." "So you'll have your dessert

one of these days. Catch you later." But he would never catch Bozzone, thought Shaw, not when he didn't know the right words. Like when he overheard Ms. Davies in Market Research mention

, and he thought it had something to do with an S&M web site. Good thing he was able to pass it off as a joke. His office door burst open. "I arrive with

, as is my wont!" It was the blathering assistant executive manager of the division. "Shaw, my good man! Time to do some real work!" Shaw nodded, pushing aside some papers. "The firm has

interests, I don't have to tell you that, . . . but this is a tad unusual even for us!" As Fisk rattled on, Shaw wondered again

how he would ever get ahead in the
company. "But there's no reason that

ec·lec·ti·cism   has to be a dirty word in today's market.
We have an excellent opportunity to

e·clipse   our closest rivals, provided we find the
right synergistic mode and can match
our client's needs to our solutions. Now
that we've hooked up with SunWorks,
with their slogan about building an

e·clip·tic   that will encompass our every I.T. need – "
"Sun who?" "Oh, sorry. You weren't
supposed to know that. Need-to-know
basis, you understand. Like our deal
with that group studying

ec·lo·gite   formation in Antarctica, all about plate
tectonics. Can't say more." "What?"
"We're optimizationizing their whole
business plan and retrieval process, but
it's need to know." "But –" "It's like that

ec·logue   , when Spenser writes, 'Shepheards
delights he dooth them all forsweare.'
Really, I'd love to tell you more."
Shaw's door opened a crack; then shy
Phyllis slipped inside, like a larva after

e·clo·sion   , too timid to lift her gaze. "You have the
strategy for the Wuzzupp account?"
"Who, me?" asked Shaw, confused.
"No, me," said Fisk, patting Shaw's
wrist. "We're

eco-   potentiating their product." Phyllis
looked horrified. "You can't say that
to just *anyone*!" "Oh, of course. We're
on a strict need-to-know basis, Shaw.
It's internal bus. streamlining

72

ecol.	kinetic ROI management. Man! Sometimes I feel like I'm still in the dear old
é·cole	, with all this material to learn!" "But who or what is Wuzzupp? Or Spenser?" "Tut-tut, Shaw. Need to know, need to know. We'll touch base soon about that other project, the
e·co·lo·gi·cal	thing where we're supposed to counter-triangulate the earnings of the energy coalitions." "*What* project? *Which* coalitions?" "All in good time, Shaw, all in good time." "But what's it got to do with
e·col·o·gy	?" "Well, not *literal* ecology, of course – that wouldn't make sense, now, would it?" The asst. ex. man. and Phyllis giggled "It's more of a
econ.	ecol. sort of thing. Which reminds me: now that Gary has brought
e·con·o·met·rics	into the performance-evaluation process you and I and perhaps Gary himself will have to sit down and see how the new approach impacts your credit accruals vs. your response debits. It's a tidy
ec·o·nom·ic	system that promises to make everyone's life a lot easier." "When did all this happen?" asked Shaw, shrugging. "I don't know anything about response debits." "Well, if we correlate an
ec·o·nom·i·cal	disadvantage to an oversupply of . . . But of course! I see: Gary hasn't shared that or the new corporate citizen profiling initiative with you yet! The whole

economic geography	of the firm has radically changed, and I'm sure you'll be hearing all about it soon." He glanced quickly at Phyllis, holding herself tight by the door. "The
ec·o·nom·ics	are obvious once you –" "The Wuzzupp account? Gary's waiting." "Oh, right. First things first. So long." Shaw ran his fingers through his hair. Did you have to be a goddamn
e·con·o·mist	to make sense of things in the company now? When did all this happen? Was he the only person not to have heard? "Pro-filing initiative?" Sounded ominous. He'd better start to
e·con·o·mize	, that was for sure. His job was safe, surely. Probably. Possibly. This wasn't a good
e·con·o·my	to be turned loose into. Just then, Ted Gold popped his head into Shaw's office. "Shaw, what do you know about talks between
ECOSOL	and that consulting firm started by Devereux and Sykes?" "Who? What's ECOSOL?" "Oh, good God, man – what are you? An example of that lamentable
ec·o·spe·cies	, the company drone? Do you do any-thing but sit and twiddle your thumbs all day?" "But where did you hear . . ." "Oh, that's right. I forgot that your corporate
ec·o·sys·tem	and mine may not overlap fully, with all the continuous improvement restructuring that's been going on these last few weeks. So you haven't been told how the

ec·o·tone

between our corporate cones will substantiate and volumize production accounting and quality assurance." "No," said Shaw slowly, "I had not heard." He sighed and wondered how he as

ec·o·type

– the office dunce – was supposed to behave. "I suppose it's all being communicated on a need-to-know basis?" "Well, I thought *everyone* knew," said Gold. How does it feel when an

é·cra·seur

slowly tightens around your trachea? Or was it the esophagus? Who could remember all that stuff? Shaw glanced down at his slacks. What were they? Tan? Beige? Or was it

ec·ru

? He needed to know. He *would* know. Or perhaps he could find someone – one of the people slinking down the hall – to tell him whether he was wearing slacks or pants. And that would be

ec·sta·sy

. Had to be one or the other, right? Slacks or pants. Beige or ecru? Placks or sants? Slants or packs? He began to chant in

ec·stat·ic

fashion, until the door opened and Gary, Gold, Phyllis, Fisk, and Bozzone peered in at him. "Look, Shaw," began Gary, "there's something you need to know."

night life —— nigrescent

	Every day after sunset I experience the phenomenon called
night life	. The "night" part I will not quibble with. The "life" is more debatable, seeing what goes on among this city's denizens. I do not mean those who go timidly to bed with the
night light	on. They have no sense of what happens beyond their locked doors, their shuttered windows. Nor do they want to know. For them, it is simply a
night·long	passage without consciousness, so that they can awaken with some freshness the next morning and go about their business. Their *proper* business, I should say. What happens
night·ly	beyond their tiny shelter is not for them. Little Edwina, pale and pretty, may call out once in a while, shaken by a half-remembered
night·mare	, but Mater and Pater are beside her bed almost at once, telling her the dream is nothing, meant nothing. She'll learn the truth in due time. The young master, Percy, may hear the hoot of a
night owl	– which it may indeed be, if it is not the more equivocal sound of a transaction gone awry – only to forget about it by morning's light. Ah, birds of night!

76

Another cry comes – perhaps the

night raven , with its grand Latin name of *Nycticorax nycticorax*. But more fitting are the words of Noah Webster, who defined it as "a fowl of ill omen that cries in the night." Now the strident clip-clop of a

night·rid·er , whipping his horse, headed out on some deadly mission of intimidation. I suppose I could count myself among them, given the way I spend my

nights . But for different reasons. Enough philosophizing. My nights are for more than leisure. Here, for example, we see a middling

night school , just letting out. That one looks like a secretary, eager to get ahead in the world. A sad ambition, if she only knew. Her pallor, her dilated eyes – as if she'd dabbled with

night·shade . Shall I follow her home, watch beyond her window – my eyesight keener than any other night creature's – as she tosses aside her skirt and slip, shivers into her plain white

night·shirt ? Sad if it were spotted with blood. Still, what a coup for her to meet Lord Carfax, dead or not. No, let us see what else the night offers. Ahead, a garden with pretensions. Few would guess that

night soil , shoveled under the cover of darkness, has helped its proud flowers grow. Does

77

one scent underlie another? Pass on, pass on. Ahead, a couple sways just beyond the exit of a fashionable

night·spot   , she's giggling as she leans against him. Hungry enough for two? I can imagine their urgency in bed, the noise of springs, the rattle of coins, watch and necklace on the

night stand   , the self-satisfied cries. No, let them indulge. And let me step back within this shadow darker than other shadows as this fine constable strides past,

night stick   ready. I have no desire to cut short his career as protector of the neighborhood. Not this night. There may be other chances in the decades to come. Hungry as I am, I await the pull of the

night·tide   that will tell me *now* is the moment, that will tell me *he* or *she* is the prey. Minutes and hours have no meaning. The only meaning is the

night·time   . And in the nighttime, it will be done. Here, slinking in the shadows, is Georgie Cool, the Cheapside Cheater. There, unsteady of step, comes a painted

night·walk·er   . All I need to do is look in her face to send her screaming in panic, a runner after all! Instead, I will ignore her, with collar raised. The night is as much hers as mine. We both shy away from the

night watch   , those sturdy, upright men who cling to

the lies of genteel society, who will protect
it so savagely if they must. I wonder which

night watchman has laid his hands on my painted friend?
Has found her flesh real. Has paid what
she asks . . . or raised his fist righteously
when a price was named? And then went
home to wife and child, donned his

night·wear in the closet, and made certain the last
candle was snuffed. Ah, a wind comes
staggering down the long, dark street!
How the walkers must shiver. Even the
debutante in her satin

night·y , warm and safe in her bedroom, must
shiver. She will wonder why. I am the
reason. I have chosen. I will land on her
balcony, open the shutters with a touch.
And by the time I whisper

night·y-night in her ear, she will not know what to
think. Tomorrow, she will not believe
what she thinks she remembers. And
then she will put all thoughts away. And
there they will stay until the sky turns

ni·gres·cent , the long day dwindles, the light fades.
That is when her weakness will return.
That is when her memories will return.
That is when the night will return, and I
in its wake.

yarrow — Yazoo

A life at sea? Well, my tale's like most you'd hear. Solid land's not solid. Too treacherous. The sea's where I know where I am. But it began with the thick scent of jasmine or

yar·row

or hyacinth, who can remember? Not an excuse, mind you, but long ago, in that Arab port, when I saw that there was indeed a woman's face behind that black

yash·mak

, I made my interest known. No groping, of course, but even a half smile or a raised eyebrow can cause trouble there. It certainly did for me. Before I knew it, I was dodging the husband's

yat·a·ghan

, trying to explain that I meant no harm, only respectful admiration, that I'd be leaving town the next day, all kinds of

yat·ter

, but nothing worked. I thought I was done for. Until the man I was to know as McGhie hailed me from a dinghy that was pulling out. "You've got less life in ye than a godforsaken

yaud

!" he shouted, beckoning. Or words of that sort. So, with my enthusiastic pursuer only yards behind me, I dove into the water and swam to the boat. "Aye, ye're a

yauld

thing, no question." And I swam 'til my arms near gave out, and they helped me into the boat. On the dock, my pursuer gave a blood-chilling

yaup , but he felt he'd done his manly duty and didn't follow. Oh, I ached a good deal and did a bit of bleeding where he'd nicked me. But some

yau·pon tea and a nip of more potent stuff that McGhie supplied soon had me feeling more myself. I could stay, he said, if the captain approved and if I didn't cause the good ship to

yaw . No, I'd never, said I. So before I knew half the names of the crew, we were bound for the Japanese islands, for a city called

Ya·wa·ta . "Yawata's not so good as my water!" laughed McGhie, but that was just the first new place for me. More and more followed. I've been on ketch and

yawl , frigate and freighter, in Baffin Bay and the Celebes sea, ogled the French belles in their finery and the painted savages standing at the shore who'd

yawl at us as the ship drew nigh. No, life at sea is nothing to

yawn about – but for damn certain it makes you appreciate your sleep. That's your best friend, most of the time. And if you do your work and don't

yawp about your lousy bunk and your lousy

pay, and you manage to steer clear of scurvy and

yaws   and those exotic diseases that you can get from the wrong dalliances in port, you'll get by. Let the captain worry about the North Star or the

y-axis   as he sets our course, I just do what he says and that's fine with me. Long as he can tell the

Yaz·oo   from the Yangtze, he can count on us.

inescapable — inexplicable

"The reality, ladies and gentlemen of the press, is

in·es·cap·a·ble

. And yet the challenger refuses to see it. The economic thrust, calculated on a curve over the past three months, is,

in esse

, self-explanatory. Still, the other candidate claims that the administration's cost-of-living diagnosis has been

in·es·sen·tial

in the campaign against the worrisome trends we have identified. In truth, the impact of the president's Eight-Point Plan on our economy has been

in·es·ti·ma·ble

in its economic impact, as the polls clearly indicate. Yes, there will be the

in·ev·i·ta·ble

downturn in certain areas, as expected, but these sciences are, frankly,

in·ex·act

, and whenever humans are concerned, which is, as you know, the president's primary area of concern, to be any less committed would be

in·ex·cus·a·ble

. We have said that since this campaign began, and we will say it again and again. Simply put, it is not

in·ex·er·tion

on the part of our citizens that is fueling this economic malaise. Quite the contrary: as the president has said on several occasions, the American spirit is

83

in·ex·haust·i·ble	and must be allowed to fill this whole continent in a fashion commensurate with its appetite for the better things in life, whether actual or still
in·ex·ist·ent	in their promise of fulfillment. This, ladies and gentlemen of the press, is something the challenger has denied consistently, when he has not had the
in·ex·o·ra·ble	eye of the media upon him. Why, just last week — and you can verify this — he claimed that it was
in·ex·pe·di·ent	to untrammel the individual thirst for economic self-determination that has made this nation great. Well, our position is that although it may be
in·ex·pen·sive	to make such statements, the true cost of confining the vision of where we want to be can only be analyzed in terms of each citizen's pocketbook. Only our opponent's
in·ex·pe·ri·ence	in such matters is leading him to utter such
in·ex·pert	opinions. In contradistinction, this administration stands for — has always stood for — grappling with the leading economic indicators that have an
in·ex·pi·a·ble	impact on the American citizen who wants to see his or her way through. To suggest otherwise is simply
in·ex·plain·a·ble	. The fact of the matter is, there may be a difference between what has occurred

in actual economic terms and what is simply an

in·ex·pli·ca·ble   misapprehension of perceived reality within the parameters we have struggled to establish for four years. Thank you."

Lohengrin —— lollygag

Lo·hen·grin led a rather sheltered life, fitting for a Knight of the Holy Grail. So when he had attained a certain age, he realized that he had never even seen his own

loin bared, let alone a woman's. Which presented a problem. What, for example, lay beneath one's

loin·cloth , and how did his compare to some other hearty young man's? He felt vaguely that Lancelot might have been able to tell him, but he was currently exiled beyond the

Loire , for what the king's press office called "indiscretions." And Pop Parsifal would be no help, believing that one should always think pure thoughts. How about

Lo·is , Yvain's comely niece? For had he not glimpsed her by the river last week as knights bathed after a skirmish? "Oops, wrong turn," she had said, but continued to

loi·ter while she tried to gauge her direction by the sun. Or so she had insisted later. Well, perhaps she combined the guile of

Lo·ki with the smile of a McDonald's counterperson. But she might be able to teach him a little of what he yearned to know. So he went to

loll by the same river, taking off his sword

to get a little more comfortable. Then he
saw a glint in the trees nearby: a telescope?
"Just trying to get a fix on

Lol·land

, that's all," called Lois. "Or Mont
Blanc. Anyway, just trying to broaden
my sense of geography." She climbed
down to join him. "Whew, that's some

lol·la·pa·loo·za

you've got there. Happy to see me, eh?"
"I beg your pardon?" "Oh, come off it,
Grinny. Only a Sunday-School

Lol·lard

wouldn't know what I'm talking about.
Care for a swim in the altogether? You
show me your John Thomas, I show you
my

lol·li·pop

d'amour. Sounds fair, my knight soon-
to-be-out-of shining armor, I hope? Race
you to the water." And thus did doughty
Lohengrin thrash and

lol·lop

to the riverside, casting aside all raiments
of modesty. There, baring her ivory
bosom, stood Lois. "Better than any

lol·ly

in the purse?" she cooed. She dropped
her gown. "Verily, I am speechless." "It's
not your speech I want, chum. Let's not

lol·ly·gag

." And thus did the knight erring learn
the secrets of a wholly different grail.

Nebraska — negotiation

From *Business Is My Business: The Autobiography of America's Favorite Corporate Leader*, Vol. V: "The SterlingCorp Years." As Told to Mitch Lattimore: How did a naïve kid from

Ne•bras•ka

end up leading some of our nation's greatest companies? It's still hard for me to comprehend. Truly, I never expected to have my own jet (three, actually) and a home like the one built by

Neb•u•chad•nez•zar

for his homesick wife. Sure, mine's in Aspen, but I'd stake my life's savings that the view beats Mesopotamia any day of the week! The sky is incredible. Nothing's more soothing than looking at a

neb•u•la

through my little home telescope, which Professor Vessalius personally designed for me. Now, as I've noted many times in this account, my kind of smarts ain't the kind that can explain the

nebular hypothesis

or anything so abstruse. No, I'm just a Nebraska kid who got lucky and who had the right kind of people around for help. And sometimes when I try to sum up what I bring to the table, I tend to

neb•u•lize

things, and I end up not saying what I meant to say! But let's be clear about one thing: in the high-stakes world of big corporations, you can't have

neb•u•los•i•ty

at the top. No, you need someone with a firm idea of where the corporation is going – and is *meant* to go. As Winston Churchill put it, "The price of greatness is responsibility." So no

neb•u•lous

notions that will only scare the stock holders! The greatness of Churchill awes me. An incredible mind. And as I've said many times before, I'm not

nec•es•sar•i•ly

the smartest guy in the room – not with Barney and Seth to keep me honest! – but I know how to do what's

nec•es•sar•y

, especially in a crisis. If you don't have the stomach to make the hard decisions, you're in the wrong line of work. Some eggheads believe that chaos – or at least near-chaos – is a

necessary condition

of business. Nothing, they'll tell you, gets done properly without a sharp awareness of both potentials and limitations. But I'm not an advocate of

ne•ces•si•tar•i•an•ism

, which holds that human will isn't free. The hell it isn't! Tell that to all the regular guys and gals who have worked long hours in the companies I've headed over the years. Circumstances will

ne•ces•si•tate

some tricky choices – we all know that – but those are the fine folk who *chose* to work for me and my board and my managers. So the will to work is definitely

ne•ces•si•tous

, and the results are self-evident in every proud smile you see on the faces of our rank and file. Sure, sometimes

ne•ces•si•ty

can be a mother, but if you know what

to do, it becomes just one more opportunity for advancement! Many, many years ago, I was fishing on the

Nech•es River in the great state of Texas, and I was feeling very glum. I'd had to downsize Speculor and put many fine employees out of work, and the press was roasting me. "You sure are getting it in the

neck ," said my fishing companion, Al Dunlop. But then he added something I never forgot, quoting Churchill: "When the eagles are silent, the parrots begin to jabber." Sure, sometimes your

neck•band is going to feel too tight, but you've just got to stand up to the pressure. And sometimes you say, "the hell with them," and to spite the carpers you put on a fancy

neck•cloth just like the ones Beau Brummell used to wear. Sure, there's pressure wherever there's responsibility. A student of history, I stop to consider what someone like Jacques

Nec•ker , the finance minister of France, had to go through in the years leading up to the French Revolution! Mind you, everyone who knows me knows I'm more comfortable in faded jeans and a

neck•er•chief , not one of Beau's fancy outfits or Jacques's breeches! And you'll never see me doing something in public like

neck•ing with a starlet, like some publicity-hungry developers and media moguls.

On the other hand, the day I signed my contract with SterlingCorp, I bought my wife a

neck•lace

. Nothing gaudy, but I was photographed coming out of the shop on Rodeo Drive – Gucci, I think – and the press had a field day! Good thing they couldn't get a shot of how it looked on Elise, with the

neck•line

of her dress! That's reserved for Papa! But we've spent way too much time on

neck•piece

fashion, and there are many, many things I've learned along the way that I'd like to share with you. And if you'll allow me to

neck-rein

you readers for a spell, I've got some other true stories that you may enjoy. So kick off those shoes and loosen your

neck•tie

. Lord knows this ain't no

necktie party

, unlike some unpleasant events that used to take place in my home state back in the wild days! As Churchill once said "If you are going through hell, keep going." Believe me, you don't need any

neck•wear

on a ride like that! But let me tell you about taking over at SterlingCorp. From the outside, it looked like a very solid organization. But was I surprised! Two days on the job, I felt like a

nec•ro-

scopist, examining the living dead! Almost nothing was functioning properly! Fortunately, Manny, my lawyer, had negotiated a very sound and competitive contract, and the

nec•ro•bi•o•sis I discovered would never hurt me. But that's never what it's all about. First off, I had to change the culture of the place. Much too much reverence for the old ways, the old managers – basically

ne•crol•a•try . If there's one thing I'm known for, it's never glorifying the past – *anyone's* past! So first thing, I had to lay off most of the upper and middle managers. Some hotheads said the list read like a

ne•crol•o•gy , but as someone once said about making an omelet, you've got to break the eggs. And you didn't need to engage in

nec•ro•man•cy to know that the former executives had it in for me the moment I joined the sinking ship and tried to right it. I've never had much taste for

nec•ro•pha•gia , so I'll let those unfortunates mutter darkly and grumble in their shadowy holes. One of them – I'm sure you know who I mean – made something of a stink a few years back with his own version of

nec•ro•phil•i•a , doing an unsavory rehash of the necessary actions I took at the time. Strange, but I didn't see his book on the *Times* bestseller list! Still, in a position like the one I held, you can't suffer from

nec•ro•pho•bi•a , either. You have to deal with the past, deal with the unfortunates who could not face the future – and that's what I did. Sure, the

ne•crop•o•lis	became rather full, but if not for the radical surgery I performed, all of SterlingCorp would have gone under. That it lasted 30 more months under my leadership is a miracle, as any fair-minded
nec•rop•sy	of its remains would clearly show. Never have Churchill's words rung more true: "You have enemies? Good. That means you've stood up for something, some time in your life." The
ne•cro•sis	I found was extensive – and growing by the hour. Swift, certain action was demanded. I firmly believe that the
ne•crot•o•my	I performed will stand up under any scrutiny. Nor is there any reason for ambulance-chasing attorneys to be involved. At any rate, I brought Sterling-Corp two additional years of life. It was time for
nec•tar	— or Champagne, if you prefer! Some of you may recall the reports about my compensation package, based on leaks from Elise during our unfortunate divorce proceedings. Oh, she was certainly a
nec•tar•ine	, delicious in season, but hard as a stone at other times! I wish her the best, now that we've simmered down, even if her
nec•ta•ry	has dried up some in the intervening years, so to speak. Still, I hear she's enjoying life with that car salesman in Wichita,
Ned	Something-or-Other. But back to the temporary furor in the press: in addition

	to the usual meaning of salary or wages, the
N.E.D.	defines *compensation* as "something that compensates for an undesirable state of affairs." Believe me, folks, nothing could provide true compensation for my time at SterlingCorp! I went to
Ne•der•land	for a well-deserved vacation while my private affairs were hashed out in the press. There I met my future wife, Britt,
née	De Jong, who offered the tender comfort I sorely needed then. The press complained about the seasons tickets I had to the Yankees and to the Metropolitan Opera, never mentioning the
need	a CEO has to entertain prospective clients in a fitting manner. Nor did they mention that I returned the tickets to the New York City Ballet! Selective reporting indeed! A free press is, I know, a
need•ful	commodity in today's world. God bless 'em when they do what they're intended to do. But the piteous
need•i•ness	the press has for sensationalism serves to undermine its legitimacy. No CEO could ever get away with the stuff the papers pull. Well, a life lesson: You make the big bucks, you get the
nee•dle	. Understood. Let's move on. Another item that somehow piqued the interest of the gossipmongers (thanks to dear Elise) was the aquarium the corporation supplied me. It was full of beautiful

nee·dle·fish   , koi, cichlids, crosshatch triggerfish, palestripe podfish, rainbows, dragonfish, you name it. What can I say – I find it soothing to look at them. Next came the fuss about the giant

nee·dle·point   we had prepared for our wedding, Britt and I, copied from the Unicorn Tapestries at the Cloisters. Yes, it took several highly skilled craftspersons a long time to create, and the gold thread,

need·less   to say, was expensive – but to equate this gift of love with the outrageous shenanigans of people like Kozlowski and Welch is ridiculous! It's like equating a tiny

needle valve   with a huge valve on a nuclear submarine! Or a plain old

nee·dle·wom·an   with an entire clothing factory! And I defy anyone to disparage the excellence of the

nee·dle·work   in our authorized copy. I should add that Britt later asked for custody of the needlepoint during our divorce proceedings, but the judge sided with me, thank God! I

need·n't   dwell on these inconsequential personal matters, but let me quote that towering figure Churchill: "All men make mistakes, but only wise men learn from their mistakes." I'm still trying! My daily

needs   , of course, are few, but the corporation wisely provided 20 years of a rent-free duplex in Manhattan for special oc-

casions, from which I could put in a good word here and there. By no means am I a

need•y   person. I will have a potato or a

neep   for dinner as readily as Kobe beef, and never complain. But over the years I've found that the evil tongue

ne'er   tires of wagging. Totally in keeping with the packages of other Fortune 500 CEOs, SterlingCorp also provided me golf club memberships to Augusta and Pine Valley. Am I a selfish

ne'er-do-well   to require the best in modern computers for my office? How else in this day and age do we communicate – and, more importantly, make deals that benefit our company *and* our nation? There's nothing

ne•far•i•ous   in that. And Monique Gall – who became my wife – was the obvious person to redecorate the duplex. The corporation had no objections. And speaking of Monique, the so-called

Nef•er•ti•ti   Scandal is a tempest in a teapot. As many readers of the tabloids will recall, for her 25th birthday, I arranged to have a bust of the famous queen carved out of ice. You'd think I had invaded the

Ne•fud   desert with Israeli tanks! How the press liked to dwell on the fact that Stolichnaya Elit streamed from the queen's mouth. As if our guests didn't deserve the best! Is the press's motto "Go

neg.	"? Sometimes it seems so. Funny, but I don't recall hearing about how, after the event, the bust was delivered to a Bronx orphanage, where it stayed until it melted. As an American, I would never
ne•gate	the important role of the press – even these doggone bloggers who seem to delight in making mischief! Yes, they have to keep the rulers in line. No question. But the degree of
ne•ga•tion	you find in just opening the morning paper is astounding! Every executive is portrayed as a scoundrel – or a scoundrel in training! There's no trace of the mythical cult of the CEO these days, when
neg•a•tive	coverage is the rage. There's so much of it, in fact, I sometimes think the whole nation could run on its
negative electricity	! But in some ways, all it takes is a strong person to wield a pen of his own and put that nice, broad stroke down the middle of the
negative sign	and turn it into a plus sign. And that's what a corporate leader has to do these days to get beyond the pervasive
neg•a•tiv•ism	about business and businesspeople. Still as the great Churchill once put it, "True genius resides in the capacity for evaluation of uncertain, hazardous, and conflicting information." If you can fight
neg•a•to•ry	views in your own corporation, you can fight it anywhere. Now, I'm no chemist or physicist, God knows – I

97

barely made it out of high-school algebra!
– but it seems that for every

neg•a•tron   there's a corresponding positron. I look
to the example of Israel, which has
worked hard for years to reclaim
the desert land in the

Ne•gev   region. Why? Because the people
believe! And that's something that our
wordy commentators in the news today
seem to

neg•lect   — belief. Faith. The possibility of success.
Imagine a CEO who was

neg•lect•ful   of such a quality – he wouldn't last
more than a few months. You have to
project trust and leadership and, yes, faith
in our cause. In my mind, you can keep
the seductive vamp of negativity in her

neg•li•gee   . Give me good old Betty Crocker, her
face shining with positive thoughts.
That's one reason I – like many executives
– believe in stock options. We're putting
our faith in our own company! It's

neg•li•gence   to do otherwise. If we run the ship onto
the reefs of debt and mismanagement,
we have been supremely

neg•li•gent   , and we go down with the ship. It's
always been that way. Sure, there is
often some kind of

neg•li•gi•ble   life jacket for the captain of the ship, but
that's customary as well. Any captain –
on the real seas or in the corporate world
– needs to know that his ship is sound.

That's hardly a

ne•go•ti•a•ble

matter – and I've been blessed with a lawyer like Manny. There was some fuss when it came out that he arranged free air travel for me in the company jets for the next 20 years, but that's why we

ne•go•ti•ate

these packages. An uncertain CEO is a dangerous CEO. I sometimes think that's why Monique and I divorced during my time with Excellicity Unlimited. But there's no agreement without

ne•go•ti•a•tion

. Try it, folks. As for me, although some have called me a grizzly, I can assure you that, with some Godiva truffles and Veuve Clicquot within easy reach, I'm actually a big teddy bear!

obliquity — oboe

Riley despised capitalism, and he saw no need for

ob·liq·ui·ty . He despised the upper classes, their hypocrisy, the simpering music they listened to in their decadent symphony halls. All those things he sought to

ob·lit·er·ate with a bomb one afternoon. But as he moved the evil contraption into his VW Rabbit, he happened to trip — and blew himself to

ob·liv·i·on . When he awoke, he found himself in a large concert hall as the orchestra warmed up. "What happened? Didn't the bomb go off?" But the people on either side were

ob·liv·i·ous to him. The trills of Signorina Brunetti, the Italian Nightingale, made him cringe. The pizzicato pricked his brain. "Answer me, you sore on society's ass!" His neighbor merely pointed to an

ob·long wooden box, some seven feet long, that lay in the aisle on the plush carpet. "What's the big idea, you anachronistic drone?" yelled Riley. And more such

ob·lo·quy spewed from his mouth. Surprisingly, his fingers tight around his neighbor's neck brought no response. Riley found the rising bleats and fanfares increasingly

ob·nox·ious   and dashed for the exit. There was, however, no exit. A skull-headed attendant
gestured to a nearby seat. "And now, our
fourteen-hour concerto for

o·boe   , cello, and annoying tinkly noises,"
announced the famous dead conductor.
Riley shrieked. And shrieked.

rattrap — Rawalpindi

When this critic arrived at Chez Veronique, he was not prepared in the least to find it a veritable

rat·trap

. Most peculiar, given the Olympian prices it charges for, at best, pedestrian fare. So, after entering the

rat·ty

vestibule, one is greeted by a

rau·cous

noise, more than the usual clatter of dishes and silverware: it sounded like the caterwauling of a bunch of

raun·chy

sailors on shore leave. This, I was informed, was the evening's entertainment, Plaid Scimitar, performing Third World funk and polka. If only I had had some potent

rau·wol·fi·a

to throw among them! So, seated at a rickety, scarcely spotless table, I was left for what seemed hours to scan a scrawled menu and permit the so-called music to

rav·age

my ears. Meanwhile, I sampled the supposedly fresh-baked bread. A terrible mistake: Did my colleague at the *Post* really

rave

about it? My waiter announced the specials so quickly and off-handedly that I was left to

rav·el the threads for myself. Had he really said scallops with beets in a chocolate sauce? As I pondered my choices, a travesty of

Ra·vel 's *Bolero* swelled around us — Plaid Scimitar going for the gold: sitar, xylophone, and tambourine playing lead. If only there were a mountain or at least a

rave·lin between us! My waiter brought some dun-colored string cheese for me to nibble on, but the

rav·el·ing itself took nearly all my energy. Stuck together with mucilage, perhaps? Then the waiter returned to explain he had los my order. Another unforeseen

rav·el·ment? Or should one have expected as much? At last, my appetizer came. To my dismay, it looked like a barely plucked

ra·ven lying stunned on a bed of sallow lettuce. I slipped it under the table. By this time, I was prepared to

rav·en the bread, but there seemed to be some visitors from the Blattaria family scuttling in and around it, as if

rav·en·ing for mites. And I — I, who have dined on the best food from New York to

Ra·ven·na , from Paris to San Francisco — was close to weeping. Still, by the time my order came at last, I was

rav·e·nous	; but what landed on my table, oozing blood and still (I thought) pulsing, seemed more like the
rav·in	of some particularly sadistic Bengal tiger. I looked around, in vain, for a
ra·vine	into which I could toss it. Had this restaurant really been the occasion for the fulsome
rav·ing	of my colleague from the *Gazette* . . . or was it mere lunacy heightened by food poisoning? It was time to reconsider: "Do you have, perchance,
ra·vi·o·li	in a simple Bolognese sauce?" I asked, near despair. "Ravioli?" "You've heard of it?" He nodded, not quite convinced. At this point, I was prepared to
rav·ish	a platypus to receive something edible. Then the dish arrived. To my embattled senses, it was, I admit,
rav·ish·ing	, even though I suspect it was straight out of a can of Chef Boyardee. But I also suspect it was the only entree in the place that was not
raw	and/or maggoty. In sum, Chez Veronique is the closest thing you will find in our city to a mess tent in a refugee camp in
Ra·wal·pin·di	. One can safely say that adventurous diners — if they survive — will undergo an experience they may never forget.

where — whicker

	"So tell me, do you have any idea
where	we are?" "None." "Well,
where·a·bouts	, at least?" "I cannot say with any great semblance of accuracy. But
where·as	we were traveling due west for several leagues,
where·at	we executed a turn to the left and gained access to this road
where·by	we hope to reach our present destination, it is my considered guess that . . ." "But
where·fore	are we proceeding leftward?" "Because leftward in this case is southerly. If the direction
where·from	we were traveling was north, and the town
where·in	we were staying previous to embarking upon our expedition is known to be northerly, and the town
where·in·to	we hope to journey is by common consent known to be southern in relation to the aforesaid town . . ." "I am not altogether convinced that I know
where·of	you speak." "Look! Surely you can see that the road
where·on	we are traveling is going south . . ."

"But does it follow that

where·so·ev·er the road travels, we must travel as well?
The bosky stretch

where·through we have but lately passed seemed neither
northerly nor southerly . . . to me, that
is." "But if the town

where·to we journey is indeed southerly, then
surely it follows that the direction

where·un·to we go is south." "Not, however, if we
were coming from the south already,

where·up·on our direction taken would be northerly,
despite the town's essential southernness.
It seems to me, thus, that

wher·ev·er we go depends on however we go, and
as we seem to lack the funds

where·with to hire a guide, we must brave all these
thorny questions ourselves." "True. If
we had the

where·with·al , we wouldn't have to burden ourselves
thus. Ah, to be rich, to be chauffered, to
be able to sail one's shining

wher·ry down the golden stream!" "But there's
no stream here!" "I was speaking figura-
tively, if you must know, trying — vainly,
it seems — to

whet your imagination." "It is, rather, a question of

wheth·er	your figurative speech was effective and understandable, given a lack of sufficient context." "I see I'd need an actual
whet·stone	to sharpen your dulled literary perceptions Oh? And now you
whew	, do you?" "And why not whew when your inadequacies shine forth so clearly Your images are as thin and runny as
whey	." "Well, at least I'm not a
whey·face	, unlike some people I know." "Oh, and
which	people do you mean, pray tell?" "I mean
which·ev·er	I mean." "An absolute tautology, my dear sir, and I assert that you stand piti-fully exposed
which·so·ev·er	excuse you may henceforth attempt. Ha, ha!" "Don't you
whick·er	at me, my good fellow — you, who can't tell north from south!" "Which reminds me, do you have any idea where we are?"

usual — Utopian

Dear Editor: I was delighted to see that my recent book on ontological defenses of private property was reviewed in your usually excellent journal. But this was not the

u·su·al

issue, if the distortions and totally unjustified attacks on my work and me are any indication. I feel much like one of the land-owners described in my study, victimized by

u·su·fruct

, that frequently misused right to enjoy all the advantages of another's property, so long as said property is not destroyed or damaged. Well, in this case, your reviewer was the

u·su·fruc·tu·ar·y

of my property – i.e., the book under review – and he has certainly damaged it, along with my scholarly reputation, with his ill-considered and ahistorical rantings. And I am scarcely a

u·su·rer

, as he has described me, for demanding full repayment for valuable documents the reviewer borrowed years ago and returned in a pitiful state. My friends know me as uxorious, not

u·sur·i·ous

, and your reviewer has long cast his "likerous ye" upon my wife. No doubt he failed to reveal this particular part of his background when he clamored to write the review. Not to

u·surp	your editorial prerogatives, but I suggest you vet your reviewers better to keep your otherwise excellent journal free of personal bias and antipathy. *The reviewer responds:* The attempted
u·sur·pa·tion	by the author of this prolix, flaccid, and ineptly argued study of one of the most fascinating areas of legal and agricultural history is, frankly, stunning. I will leave aside the matter of
u·su·ry	, because said author apparently totally misunderstood my witty metaphor. But I will not remain silent while he attempts to usurp the roles of other scholars, editors, reviewers,
usw	. Not content with writing the book, he wants to direct the review as well. Fortunately, that's not how it works in our rigorous academic system, which,
ut	*humiliter opinor* – "in my humble opinion," for the benefit of our language-limited author – is the finest in the world. Perhaps he has labored too long at his junior college in rural
U·tah	to understand the intricacies of the modern scholarly world. In the meantime, we must look elsewhere for the definitive study of the shifting views of property law. *The author responds:* I will,

ut dict. , confine myself to correcting the more egregious errors in my colleague's review, while marveling at how far he's come since his Brooklyn days. How well I remember when he spoke of "the

Ute of America" when seeking converts to his crypto-anarchist philosophy or when he'd ask me to meet him at "Toity-Toid Street" for a meal. Sad that he wasn't sure which

u·ten·sil to use in an actual, genuine restaurant! But it is not my purpose to wonder about the reviewer's attempts to distance himself from his

u·ter·ine origins or to suggest that he write his mother more than once a year. We'll leave aside the morbidly fascinating

u·ter·o- psychosociological melodrama playing in the reviewer's mind. My unparalleled study of the ways philosophers, theologians, and lawyers sought to justify land ownership was in the

u·ter·us for many years – but I should probably clarify for the reviewer that I am employing a figure of speech here and ask him not to foment insinuations about my sexuality. If he oversteps, not even

U Thant would be able to intercede peacefully between us. That said, when the reviewer, in his shoddy review, questioned my reference to the close, almost uncanny link between

U·ther

and his property, he misread. I referred not to the father of King Arthur but to the Poe character, Usher, whose "house," to remind certain people, "fell" when he did. Nor did I mean

U·ti·ca

, N.Y, properly celebrated as the home of Saranac beers, in another passage, but the ancient Phoenician city in Africa. Such historical references are normally quite

u·tile

in academic writing, and one normally expects the reviewers of academic texts to permit one to

u·ti·lise

them judiciously. My credo is not to use any such allusions unless they are both vivid and

u·til·i·tar·i·an

, as the reference was in this case. Now I know that's a very big word and it's entirely possible that the reviewer doesn't have a clue what

u·til·i·tar·i·an·ism

means – but I'm not the one who skipped college classes to go shoot pool and get drunk on wines like Bali Hai and Strawberry Hill.

The reviewer replies: There is a certain

u·til·i·ty

to the letters section of our professional journals, and I'm sure the interchanges have led to valid reassessments of the issues under consideration. But it can sometimes seem more like a

utility room

, wherein washing machines and furnaces

are going full blast, all sound and fury – and it's Shakespeare, not Faulkner, dear author – and clear thinking is lost. I can't help but notice how he spelled

u·ti·lize , going for the English spelling, because if there's one thing certain about the frustrated author of that lame book, it's that he's a snob of the first order, as I will demonstrate

ut in·fra . And I will do my

ut·most to write clearly and simply, so that he can understand. On page 433, for example, he seems to believe that

U·to-Az·tec·an is a dance craze among the leisured youth of America, not an important family of American Indian languages. But I suppose the only place where our author would be culturally comfortable is a

U·to·pi·a of his own mind, where he is everything. Would that he leave us all and go reside in some comparable place. But that, I fear, is merely a

U·to·pi·an dream on my part.
   The editor writes: I apologize to our readers. When I made my assignment, I had no idea that the author and the reviewer were brothers.

delicate — della Robbia

He saw her walking in his direction and knew he had finally reached a turning point in his life. He had to try, at least, knowing it would be a most

del·i·cate

undertaking. He might never have another chance to run his fingers through her black, electric hair. So he followed her into the

del·i·ca·tes·sen

, took his number, and inhaled the

de·li·cious

aromas of meat and cheese. He nearly salivated as he plotted his soft

de·lict

. Should he try that old ploy, mistaken identity? Might work. "Good heavens! Alexandra! After so long! What a

de·light

to see you!" "I beg your pardon, my name is . . . Marisol." "Oh, my mistake! Well, Marisol, you can call me Klaus, and I'm equally

de·light·ed

to meet you." The owner, weighing the sliced provolone, then broke in: "How

de·light·ful

for both of you, but don't disturb the other customers." Still, the strangers had their opening. The closer they were, the more she enthralled him, like a seductress, his own

De·li·lah

, and he saw no reason to

de·lim·it his euphoria. Everything about her dazzled him: he watched her eyes shine, her lips moisten, her clinging satin dress

de·lin·e·ate those twin prizes, her breasts . . . and it would be a gross

de·lin·quen·cy not to mention her walk, a proud prance that would turn the coldest misogynist into a slobbering juvenile

de·lin·quent . He felt all his scruples flee, his caution

del·i·quesce . They were meant for each other! He felt it. And, later, in his room, he found how right he was: they plunged into a shared

del·i·ra·tion of desire. Buttons, snaps — open! Shoes, clothes — off! By now, nearly

de·lir·i·ous with anticipation, they fell naked upon the bed and made flesh their every fantasy. "Oh, Klaus!" "Oh, Marisol!" At last he knew the meaning of

de·lir·i·um , the extended ecstasy in her arms. And he knew he would gladly suffer torture, deprivation, even the worst

delirium tre·mens , to be with her each evening. She trailed a ringlet of her black hair along his chest, making him catch his breath. Then he lavished such attention on her

del·i·tes·cent charms that at last she trilled and trilled like the first cuckoo of spring immortalized by

De·li·us . And then, brooking no more delay, he had his own sweet cargo to

de·liv·er . Service with much more than a smile! Having delivered, he sank with her into a nirvana of satisfaction. This, only this, had the taste of true

de·liv·er·ance . They rested, they grew hungry again for their shameless sharing, and they were primed to . . . A fearsome pounding on the door. "Hello! Got a

de·liv·er·y for Mr. Jones." More knocks, even louder. Confounded interruption! "Is that Mr. Klaus Jones?" she asked with a giggle. "Hello! It's the

de·liv·er·y man . Package for Mr. Jones." "Leave it at the door!" he barked. To her, he murmured, "We'll meet again, soon." "Where?" "In the lovers'

dell , of course. There you shall make me sing, and I shall make you sigh, and we'll disport as nymph and satyr, enough to bring a blush to

del·la Rob·bia 's sacred art."

Yes, it was easier to conduct scientific research in the old days! None of this nonsense they have to go through now. We had groups of

identical twins

to work with – treated them just fine, they saw their parents every so often, not a whimper from them – and we'd try some profoundly interesting tests. We'd undermine their sense of

i·den·ti·fi·ca·tion

, keeping them in the plain isolation ward, pipe some disorienting sounds in, then trot them out into the auditorium and ask them to

i·den·ti·fy

this or that – can't remember exactly, but it was damned important back then. All connected to the war effort, you understand. Probably shouldn't be talking about it even now. Or we'd use an

I·den·ti·kit

, one of those newfangled things at the time, for creating images of criminals, and tell the twins we were trying to discover the

i·den·ti·ty

of a vicious murderer. We'd have them help us slowly build up a face – and the face would turn out to look exactly like them! A kind of auto-

id·e·o-

accusation or what have you. Observed how they reacted under the acute stress, whether they turned on each other, and so on. Fascinating stuff! Showed them an

id·e·o·gram that was totally obscure, didn't seem to be related to anything in our known universe, and had them come up with an ur-myth to explain it. We'd grade their

id·e·o·graph·ic explanations as a team, then separate them. I don't recall all the particulars, but I think we told each twin that his sibling would suffer some kind of punishment if his

id·e·og·ra·phy was not clear and convincing. Had something to do with thinking on your feet in a foreign territory, in a crisis situation, and the War Office was desperate for facts! Back then, before all this

i·de·o·log·i·cal folderol, they respected science. Didn't have to explain and defend every damn thing you did that involved an otherwise inessential unit of the population. I'm a bit of an

i·de·ol·o·gist myself, certainly, when it comes to doing necessary work without always having to look over your shoulder. And you should have heard the claptrap we'd get from some of the twins, who'd

i·de·ol·o·gize as ridiculously as any union thug! No sense of the greater good, you understand. If there's one thing I can't abide, it's an

i·de·o·logue who refuses to see the other side, the full picture. And once

i·de·ol·o·gy enters the picture, you can forget about

good science! For example, we did a
number of interesting experiments on the

i·de·o·mo·tor   effect, when subjects make motions
unconsciously – or claim that it's uncon-
scious. Had them in straitjackets until . . .
Well, I've gabbed more than I have in a
while. See you next week?

fledgling — fleet

fledg·ling

flee

fleece

fleec·y

fleer

fleet

fleet

fleet

"Neow, watch 'ow Hi does hit," says Georgie Cool, the Cheapside Cheater, strutting about in his shiny jacket. "Yew've got lots to learn," he tells the

. "Fer one, alwise mike sure yew've got yer avenue of heskipe, so's yew kin

if yew must. A'course, the best of us prefers ta 'ave the client 'isself give 'is money tew us. Which is to say, we

'em, like, and leave 'em not knowin' what's what. Yew with me, son?" he says, rubbing the boy's

scalp. "The confidence gyme is what we calls hit. Tell you what – yew kin watch me with this next fine feller." But instead the lad breaks free and begins to

and gibber at him something horrible. "This yer wallet, mister?" he shouts at Georgie. And Georgie feels for it – it'. gone all right! So he makes a grab at the lad, who's too

by half. "Hi'll brike ev'ry bone you 'as!" says Georgie, steaming hot, but all the while he's coolly considering all he could do with a

of clever scamps like this one. "Cor! They'd be fleet of feet and

in flight," he thinks. "Well, now, me lad, let's yew and me see if we can't form us a contractization. What say?"

glyptograph —— goat

Chapter 1. "*Pardon*, monsieur, are you the renowned Harvard symbologist who has starred in a number of unaccountably popular novels?" "Yes, that's me." "Have you ever seen a

glyp·to·graph   like this?" The stranger leaned over Glandon's desk. In his palm was a signet ring with intricate markings. "What do you make of it?" "Looks about 10

gm.   , give or take a few. What's it mean?" "That's why I came to you – although it was *très difficile* to find you. I fear there is no symbology department at Harvard. I am Bertrand Chabot,

G.M.   ." "General manager?" "No, Grand Master." "Chess?" "No – Knights Templar. I thought you would know, considering my plain white tunic with a red cross." "Look, M. Chabot, I'm not a

G-man   or C.I.A. agent. I can't know everything. You don't see a Knight Templar every day." He folded his arms, looking professorial in his tweed jacket. "So where did you find it?" "A man with a

Gmc.   accent called at my unlisted number and told me to look under my vanity. *Et voilà*, there it was, affixed with Scotch Tape!" "Please, no product placement. When did the call come?" "2:37 p.m.,

GMT	, *je crois*. Why do you ask?" "Because in thrillers, it's always better if we're racing against the clock." "And that is why the chapters are so short?" "Everyone's a critic," said Glandon, about to
gnar	. "What think you of this?" asked Chabot, brandishing a shiny black stick about three feet long, somewhat twisted with a
gnarl	at one end. "It looks much like the Staff of Ptah," said Glandon, peering at it. "In actuality," said Chabot, "it's my Irish cousin's shillelagh." This time, Glandon let out an exasperated
gnarl	. "M. Chabot, I fear you are wasting my time!" "*Attends*, my dear professor of symbio- . . . synthe- . . . *Merde*! What was that discipline of yours?" "If you don't take your damn
gnarled	cudgel out of here and let me get back to my research on the covert meanings of the Subaru logo . . ." "But don't we always end a chapter with a cliffhanger?" Suddenly, the door flew open. With a
gnash	of teeth and a gasp of surprise – or perhaps the other way around – Glandon and Chabot stared at the open door. Chapter 2. Buzzing faintly, a
gnat	flew into the room, tantalizingly slow. "Phew," said Glandon after some brisk
gnath·ic	movement. "For a sec I thought it was

one of my students, angry about my delay in returning mid-terms." "*Oui*," said Chabot sympathetically, "few creatures are more fierce. Any

gnathic index would surely suggest that the typical student is descended from meat-eating savages, just waiting to stuff his horrible

gna·thite with bloody flesh. But to business, please! *Tout le monde* knows you are the most accomplished interpreter of symbols that has ever lived – and handsome to boot." "Your

gna·thon·ic prattle is a bit much, but you're basically correct." "*Bien*, then let me tell my story. A rolled scrap of paper was inserted in this odd ring, and on it was scrawled these words: 'fear the opistho

-gnathous one.' *Enfin*, I have no idea what it means!" "Well, as a Harvard professor, I know that 'opisthognathous' means 'with a receding jaw.' But it's obviously in code." Excited, he began to

gnaw on his knuckle. Then he grabbed a pen and blank sheet of paper and started writing the letters of 'opisthognathous' in a circle. "That looks like fun," said Chabot,

gnaw·ing on his own knuckle. "So what do you think?" said Glandon. "It's an anagram, but which? 'Hang us, that is poo'? 'San Pogo, thou shit'? Or 'His hot soup tango'?" "My head may be nothing but

gneiss	," said Chabot, "but what if there really is an opisthognathous one whom I must fear?" "M. Chabot, if we could talk all this out while drinking Peroni and stuffing our faces with
gnoc·chi	, you'd understand. But it's just about time for another shock that will make our readers turn to the next chapter." Just then, a shadow loomed in the doorway. Chapter 3. A long-haired albino
gnome	burst into the office, waving a fearsome ax. "*Sacré bleu!*" gasped Chabot, seeing the gnome's receding jaw. But before the stranger could act, Glandon felled him with his electroshock gun. "A
gnome	we can all live by: *semper paratus*. Mind you, the use of the phrase precedes the Coast Guard by many centuries. According to da Vinci, whose encrypted notebooks are always
gno·mic	, it was a password used by some radical groups of early Christians who hid in the catacombs. With their staunch faith, they always considered themselves prepared to die. And when the
gno·mon	of a sundial casts its shadow in a certain way –" "Which would then make it a
gno·mon·ic	shadow?" asked Chabot in confusion. "Of course! Please don't interrupt my spontaneous displays of arcane knowledge." "I regret, Professor Glandon. I

trust my downfallen physio

-gnomy adequately reflects my shame? But you do know that his name was not da Vinci? That's simply his provenance." "Oh, don't bring that up again," replied Glandon testily. "What matters is the

gno·sis imbued in his life's work, which stands the test of time." "Speaking of time, is it time yet for another cliffhanger chapter ending? My prog

-gnosis is that one is very near." Abruptly, the gnome sprang to his feet. He thrust his fist in Glandon's direction, middle finger straight up, then dashed from the room. Chapter 4. "Ah, the old

gnos·tic sign of shared secret knowledge." "Shouldn't you call the police?" asked Chabot. "Ha! Don't you know how easy it is for a long-haired albino gnome to blend into a crowd? . . . But

Gnos·ti·cism is seeming more and more like the key to this mystery. If I can solve it and save the world at the same time, my next book will lift the United States

GNP ." "And will there be another main character confined to a wheelchair?" "Don't know." "Does a wheelchair symbolize a crippled literary imagination?" "No, that's represented by a pink

gnu wearing a crown of thorns and grasping a sagging scepter." Glandon sprang

124

toward the door. "There's no time to lose!" "But where will you

go
?" asked Chabot, panting as he tried to keep up. After all, Glandon once fell from a plane flying over Rome, got to his feet, and started running as if he'd suffered a mere annoyance. "I will

go
to the ends of the earth if necessary," the symbologist shot back. "But first, I desperately need a latte." "*Moi aussi*. And is there what the military calls a

GO
that the chief villain in your book will again be the most implausible person, hiding behind a veil of virtue?" Glandon halted at the coffee shop – but the door was closed!
Chapter 5. Somewhere in

Go·a
, a figure stood gazing at the Arabian Sea. He spoke rapidly into a cell phone. "Has it begun? . . . Good." Meanwhile, Glandon pushed the door of the coffee shop. It opened! "Well, I'll be a lame

go·a
! Business as usual! After you." He did not have to

goad
Chabot, who entered with alacrity. They took their seats at a table, oblivious of the long-haired albino gnome in the back, hunched over his mochaccino. "So, M. Chabot, I have the

go-a·head
from you to pursue this mystery until it

unravels, no matter where it leads?"
"*Bien sûr!*" "Even if it leads into the
very core of the Knights Templar?"
"Professor Glandon, my

goal remains as firm as ever. But how will
you proceed?" Glandon took a sip of
his coffee. "First, I think we must reject
the traditional Asian view of the balance
of forces, yin and yang,

goal·keep·er and ball." "Not goalkeeper and goal?"
"Whatever. No, the pattern of thought
behind this plot is tri-, not bi-, what the
West has long symbolized as rock, paper,
scissors. If the rock stands for the

goal line , then we must proceed in the manner of
paper. But we may then encounter a

goal·post which, in the manner of scissors, will
cut our paper. So if . . ." Suddenly, M.
Chabot spit his coffee out, staggered to
his feet, and uttered a curse.
Chapter 6. "*Mon dieu*! It is as if they mixed

Goa powder into the coffee grounds! Too bitter! I
must speak to the manager." He stamped
off toward the counter. But Glandon had
had enough of M. Chabot's antics. The
man had gotten his

goat once too often. "The hell with this so-
called Grand Master," he muttered. "I
can spend my time better correcting the
damn mid-terms."
The End.

Monsignor — monstrance

Mon·si·gnor O'Brien prayed desperately in the confessional, his soul, he felt, near drowning in a

mon·soon of forbidden desires. Still the whisper came, her voice, through the grille. If she only knew! He imagined her ripening breasts, her silken panties, and underneath — O God! — her

mons pu·bis . Drive out these thoughts, Lord! Yet she continued to enumerate her sins: the soft voice, the hesitant sensualities of young ladies. Is it Miss Fremont? Only a

mon·ster or the vilest of hypocrites would seek to take advantage. For him, darkness was without — and within. At last, when hope was nearly extinct, she left. In the chapel, the

mon·strance shone like a beacon. He knelt and crossed himself in thanks.

Kt — kudzu

"Is this a @$#&ing Plaid Scimitar world tour or isn't it?" asked Tommy, hurling his beer bottle across the aisle of the plane. "What about London and Paris? Huh?" "Let's try King's

Kt takes B. Check," said Sam, moving his piece, as quiet during chess as he was animated behind the drum set. "You @$#&ing playing with yourself, man?" demanded Tommy. "If I had a 50

kt. bomb, I'd drop it on Unlimited Creative Artists for booking these crap sites. Who do they think we are – @$#&ing Menudo or something? We've got a

K.T. from Malta, and not everyone gets one of those." "I forget what that means," said Bruno, the bass player, looking up from his Harry Potter. "Knights Who Love Tits?" "And don't forget

Kua·la Lum·pur ," added Tommy, "which gave us a Fellowship Medal . . . probably for keeping the crowd's attention while the bosses looted the treasury!" "Yeah, meet the new boss, ek cetera." "Below, see

Ku·ban River, one of important rivers of North Caucasus," came the pilot's voice. "@$#& him," muttered Tommy. "Is there any damn Paris or London down there?" "The Caucasus – is that where

Ku·blai Khan

was from?" asked Bruno. "And all that golden palace stuff and geishas, ek setera." "@$#& it, Bruno, if you say 'EK setera' one more time, I'm going to stuff this @$#&ing

ku·chen

down your @$#&ing throat!" said Tommy. "Not that I want to waste it – this stuff is good!" "Got raisins in it?" asked Sam poring over the chess set. "I hate raisins. Remember

Ku·ching

, when they were mixed in with the noodles?" "Yeah, Kuching, who can forget, Sam? They almost took the medal back after you trashed the place." "But, Tommy Boy, it was all smiles and

ku·dos

at the airport." "Yeah, when we got *on* the plane, Sam. @$#&ing glad to see us leave." He picked up a black Takamine and strummed it. "Oh, baby," he sang, "you're as sleek as a

ku·du

, gonna hunt you down with my hoodoo, 'cause *no*-body moves me like you do." "That's a shitty rhyme, man," said Tyler, the lead guitarist, roused from his nap. "@$#& you, man. You got

kud·zu

in your ears, like all you Southern boys." "Bite me, man. . . . Say, when we gonna see some of the red-hot French mam'selles?"

memento —— Memphis

"You say I must remember," said Lee, "but remember what *you* want me to remember. Where is the sense in that? I have memories of my own." "So is this tarnished arm bracelet a

me·men·to

, something that reminds you of *your* past?" asked Howe with a laugh. "A bracelet – from when? Were *you* an Egyptian noble at one time? Sheer vanity! What you need is a

me·men·to mo·ri

to remind you of the *facts* of life. A skull, perhaps, or the photo of a companion long departed." "Departed doesn't always mean dead, my friend, as the 'Man of Sorrows' painting by Hans

Mem·ling

shows us – Christ crucified, his side pierced, and yet he is back to greet us." "You worry me!" "Why? Because I remember the broad streets of Thebes and the music produced by the Colossi of

Mem·non

when touched by the first rays of the sun? Because I remember how it felt to be sold into slavery by Nebuchadnezzar's victorious troops? Or to see the descending blade of the Aztec priest?" "Here's a

mem·o

, Lee. Enough delusions! You're living in suburban America, not the ancient world. . . . Coming to the game on Saturday?" "We'll see." Once his friend had gone, Lee considered his last

mem·oir   , which recounted the meeting between Hannibal and the traveler who told him that the Romans would never suspect an invasion from the north. What

mem·o·ra·bil·i·a   had he brought back that time? A Carthaginian sword – not that anyone in this town or even at the university museum would ever recognize it, appreciate how

mem·o·ra·ble   it truly was. Now it was stored safely, away from prying eyes. And the bracelet Howe had ridiculed? Lee didn't have time today to take it to the storage room he rented. So he began a

mem·o·ran·dum   to himself: "Arm bracelet; gold; belonging to the hierophant of Ptah, 6th Dynasty." Not that he could forget! Two days later high up on the ladder as he cleared the gutters of leaves, he slipped and fell. His

me·mo·ri·al   service was brief. Except for Howe and one or two acquaintances from his office, few people had known him. Some days after that, Howe learned that he had been left a box of trinkets. It was only on

Memorial Day   , months later, that he could bring himself to look more closely at what the box contained. But on this day of all days, it was appropriate to remember. Howe knew he was no

me·mo·ri·al·ist   who could evoke Lee's odd personality – certainly not to others – but perhaps he'd find something that would help

me·mo·ri·al·ize him in a personal way. Then he found
the arm bracelet – and the fanciful
memo. Yes, Lee was never out of character for long! Who the hell was Ptah?
Howe stared at the bracelet, as if to

mem·o·rize it. He fought against the impulse, then
. . . "Oh, give it a try!" He slipped it on
his left arm. There was a sudden onrush
of images, a confusion of colors and
sounds. Howe grabbed for the chair. A

mem·o·ry he had forgotten he'd ever had? No –
much stronger! From somewhere, he
heard – *thought* he heard – chanting in
an unknown language. He looked: it
could only be the Nile. And it was

Mem·phis , he now knew, the center of Ptah's cult.
And he knew that because . . . he would
not believe it . . . he found himself
chanting those same unknown words,
unfamiliar no more.

year —— Yeats

The letter rested in his lap. His fingers, nearly trembling, touched a corner. Invitation to the reunion. He could remember the

year

, the month, the very day he had last seen her. In the kitchen, Janet was rattling bowls, preparing to make the dough, so he jumped up and pulled out his high-school

year•book

. The pages resisted. Where was her picture? English class it was, reading something about a heart in darkness (his) and a

year•ling

, or maybe it was Shakespeare's Caesar. Her fresh scent. He had sat beside her throughout the

year•long

course, filling his notebooks with paraphrase and theory . . . when what he wanted to do was compose an invitation to the school's

year•ly

spring festival. Because she was spring: no doubt about that. Even now, his heart ached. How, at age seventeen, could he

yearn

so passionately, so innocently, for some one? And poets claimed that such

yearn•ing

ennobled the soul. Whose soul? Certainly not his. He glanced at all the

year-round activities captured in the book. But where was her picture? From fall and winter to life-giving spring. Oh, if he could only be a

yea•say•er , seeing in that progression a pattern for his life. But spring had brought only pain. From spring right back into winter, forever winter. "Honey? Have you seen our packets of

yeast in the refrigerator?" "Behind the mustard, I think," he replied. He shook his head, slowly, sadly: How could I think forever? But perhaps those were

yeast•y times — something rich came from them. Something different. Like a golden loaf? Kneading; needing. No reunion for him. Later, perhaps,

Yeats would comfort him, sharing his torment in breathtaking verse, telling him again about Maud Gonne and the old high way of love.

Zarathustra — zebec

	With a sigh, she closed the paperback copy of "Thus Spoke
Zar•a•thus•tra	." Was it ever too late to be educated? Could she summon the same dedication and enthusiasm after these years away? In the class on Africa, she'd seen images of the protective enclosure, a
za•re•ba	, made of thorn bushes. That's what she needed, to keep distractions away. But how? Then his voice: "Where the hell is my coffee?" "Get it yourself." A moment later, the bronze
zarf	that held his favorite cup came whistling at her head. Good thing he had been drinking something else before returning to his coffee. Bad aim. "Just do it. I don't want to hear a damned
zar•zu•e•la	about your dignity, your humanity, your this and that. Who brings home the damn money to keep us in this luxury?" He laughed at his own joke. "Did learning about a goddamn
z-ax•is	help me get ahead? Huh? Tell me that! Did it help me keep my job when people got tired of our product?" Saturday, past noon. He was still in his pajamas. "Dalet, hay, vav,
za•yin	," she whispered to herself, trying to stay calm. Is that the order? He shuffled

135

closer, flexing his fingers. Stay calm. "You know, I wish you'd have shown such dedication and

zeal when I was riding high," he said, leaning over the table. He touched the paperback, then pulled his hand away, as if from some leprous object. "Of course, when I was zipping from Paris to New

Zea•land with my goddamn boy-wonder boss, all I needed you for was to hang on my arm and look gorgeous when we made our entry at the openings and parties." He leaned closer. "Shit, I was a

zeal•ot for Medianistics, and what did it get me?" He gathered her hair in his hand. She closed her eyes, trying to recall images in the world history textbook. The storming of the Bastille. Athenians

zeal•ous for democracy, debating in the Assembly. The Magna Carta, a demand for rights. He was pulling her head back. Back. Barbary pirates in a swift

ze•bec , laden with plunder. "Yes, you're so enthusiastic now." The murder of Caesar. Pulling. "Aren't you?" Pulling harder now.

nocturnal — nodding acquaintance

I am responding to the editor's request
for some biographical notes from each
contributor. Kosmiq Redwing is not my
birth-name. A

noc•tur•nal

creature, like most poets, I am wary of
the unambiguous sun. The plangent

noc•turne

of dashed hopes is my song. The whole
Western tradition of hard-edged rational-
ism is, in my view,

noc•u•ous

to the soul. For how often, as one scans
the daily breakdown of facts and figures,
does one

nod

off and miss the true wonder of our
friends the newt, the condor, and the
restless cavy. In my haiku in this issue,
for example, I try to cut through all the

nod•al

complications that can grow, if we are
not careful, on our thick skulls. And,
yes, sometimes I dare hope that I have at
least a

nod•ding acquaintance

with that elusive spirit, Inspiration, who
has charged me with bringing that eva-
nescent flash of illumination to my fellows.
Shantih.

Fichte —— fiddle-faddle

Outside, the wind howled. It was as if the souls of all this dark city's dead were moaning together. Klaus sat staring at his

Fich•te , his Kant – all the dry philosophizing, frozen in these dead books. He sighed, turned a page. Then, a pebble struck the window. Throwing open the shutters, he spied a woman in a

fi•chu looking up at him, half in shadow. She gestured furtively. Was it Marisol, his dusky gypsy lover, who had kicked him out of her bed, the

fick•le thing, all because he would not sell his philosophy tomes to buy her a gift? "Go, then," she had said, baring her teeth, tossing her mane of black, electric hair. "I don't care a

fi•co for your ponderous Teutonic verbosity. Give me life! Give me honest blood and sweat! Give me your soul – or give me nothing!" "Now just a minute, Master Klaus! The real world is not so

fic•tile as you pretend." It was Marisol, peering into the cramped attic room. "It happened nothing like that! All I said is it would be nice if you bathed more than once every fortnight. Pure

fic•tion to pretend otherwise. It seems your skin is thin as well as odiferous. And I'm about as much a gypsy as you are! Must you

fic•tion•a•lize

all that happens in your life? Poor, poor child!" "Now who's fictionalizing?" he replied, throwing down his quill. "You snapped at me –" "Hopeless

fic•tion•eer

! I merely expressed my disagreement." "Snapped at me, I say, just because I happened to mention that your hair seemed drab and lifeless on this particular day." "Ah, yes – the

fic•tion•ist

at work, armed with God's memory and God's temperance. What you told me, sir, is that my hair looked like a rat's nest. Is it any wonder that I would take exception to this entirely

fic•ti•tious

explanation?" Klaus pounded his musty copy of Fichte's *Foundations*. "Then why did I describe your hair as black and electric? Is that objectionable?" Marisol hesitated. "A

fic•tive

assertion, by which you attempt to apologize for your actions. And, I must concede, a generous attempt." "Ah," he said. "Perhaps," she continued, "I will not have to go after you with that stout

fid

that you use to prop up your hopelessly uneven bookcase." "There's that to be grateful for," murmured Klaus. "I wouldn't have been much good with a b

-fid

brain!" "But let me add this," she said. "Would a character really be able to distinguish a fichu, given the darkness and the distance from the window?" "Don't

fid•dle

any more with my creation, dear Marisol," he replied evenly. "Creation? That's a rather grand way to describe some scribbles on paper!" "Better than you can do!" "Oh,

fid•dle•de•dee

, say I." "That's about all you can say," he said. "Then how about this: *she advanced on him, eyes flashing, bosom heaving.*" "To be truthful, not too bad," he said. "It's

fid•dle-fad•dle

, of course, but shows promise. Shall we read a bit more?"

I thought I was Romeo to her Juliet, peanut butter to her jelly,

dit to her dah. Yes, how naïve I was! For al along she was scheming deep in her hear to

ditch me. All is for the best, I believed at one time. God was peerless. Good would prevail. Not for me the heresy of

di•the•ism . Until my eyes were opened, and now I see that Satan, Ahriman, call him what you wish, is as powerful in our lives as the beneficent god. She greeted me with a kiss, all in a

dith•er . "No, darling," she cooed, "I heard no coughing in the closet." At ease, I looked away. It must have been then tha she poured the

di•thi•on•ic acid into my glass of wine. I drank; I tottered; I fell. "Lucille! Beloved! Can this be?" "Die, die, you toad!" she shrieked. From the closet came Raoul. They embraced. They danced and sang a

dith•y•ramb of lust. My final thought: will the Dark God permit me to haunt them the rest of their hollow lives?

career woman — carhop

Mira Rustgi glanced at her reflection in the plate glass window as she approached the company's entrance. To all appearances, a

career woman

hurrying, but not frantically, to a business appointment. Fine. Exactly what's needed. Act professional. There is a time and a place for seeming

care•free

, and she knew that North particularly frowned on uninvited levity at these meetings. Another reason to be

care•ful

: Amanda Phelps would be at the meeting, and Amanda had been training her beady eyes on her for the last two weeks. Yesterday, Mira had made a

care•less

comment about the city's shocking poverty. "And whose fault is that?" murmured Ms. Phelps. They entered the meeting room. "Wellll-comme, evvvery-onnne," said North, letting his lips

ca•ress

each syllable. He seemed to be gearing up for one of his more theatrical presentations. He made a quick flick of his Mt. Blanc pen, perhaps a

car•et

in the neat lines of notes he had on his clipboard. Not for him the more modern devices! Sometimes Mira thought he saw himself as a fierce

care•tak•er	of the Sound Old Ways, the ways that had worked for his father and grand-father. But when it came to firing an employee, North certainly knew which buttons to push. Poor Sammy
Ca•rew	! The security guards escorted him from the building, and he couldn't even e-mail some personal documents to his home computer or clear out his desk. Mira had spotted his
care•worn	face as she left that evening. He was lingering at the corner, hands in pockets looking upward every few moments, as if waiting for a sign from God. Or was he getting the courage to ask for
car•fare	? But when he caught sight of her, he ducked into the subway entrance. Suddenly Mira realized North was looking at her. "All my executives must be totally focused on getting our goods, our
car•go	to customers. We must be ready to wage war against our competitors as we solidify and leverage our place in the market place. If you can't rise to that level, get a job as a
car•hop	, and live out your pitiful life. We're not running a charity, damn it." The others, Amanda Phelps among them, were nodding enthusiastically. Mira met his glance and did not look away.

driving — drop

driv•ing

The rain never slowed him, not even a dark downpour like this one. He took

as his divine right, and he barely slackened his speed at the most dangerous corners. His jaw was set. But, after all, he was a winner, the one who'd doubled his family's fortune, the

driving wheel

behind the unscrupulous takeovers of several respected companies. "Oh, we Clarkes are quite used to rape and pillage," he once said with a laugh to a business reporter. The rain was now a gray

driz•zle

, and he pressed down on the XK's accelerator. Which had it been? A blonde. Nice figure, as he'd found when he tore off her dress and threw her over the couch. . . . His ancestors had served at

Drog•he•da

, slaughtering scores of the unwashed Irish. Later, they'd lashed some Sepoys to the mouths of cannons, to make an example of them. And in the colonial plantations, used a slave or two as a

drogue

for the company ship, to quiet the murmurs and keep their minds focused on their work. The motor hummed satisfactorily. Then, ahead, a woman in a uniform waved at him. "*À*

droit

, *monsieur*," she called out when he slowed down. No, that would take him too far out of his way. Stupid French! Still, he had to applaud the concept of

droit du sei•gneur , which he'd more or less exercised with some of the firm's more fetching girls. "Come here, darling." Opening his fly. "Now fetch!" How

droll . But this, it seemed, was not the time for

droll•er•y , not with the ditch that suddenly appeared in the road. "Damnation!" Where to? The rain was falling harder. A faded sign for an aero

-drome indicated a sharp left turn. Over a grassy stretch. Don't these people believe in keeping up their highways? I'm not a blood

drom•e•dar•y , you know! Through a row of rain-battered trees, he caught sight of water. A bay, if he remembered rightly. Where raiders of old touched shore . . . and took their pleasure. Then he spotted it — a

drom•ond , long and many-oared, with sails rippling in the wind. It must take hundreds to drive such a ship! How did it beach in this forsaken place? In this whimpering day and age? Some pseudo

-dromous homing instinct? Abruptly, the Jaguar lurched to the right. He'd been distracted by the damn ship. He gripped the steering wheel, trying to bring the bouncing car under control. There was an odd

drone coming from somewhere. Ghastly!

Braking. Finally! Then he saw them –
figures approaching from the ancient
ship, wielding spears and swords and
battle-axes. *What*? But he was no stingless

drone , no wanker without a spine. He reached
into the glovebox for the automatic he
was never without. Stupid costumers,
ghosts from the past – no matter, they'd
feel these bullets. Did they all have

drool dripping from their beards? A dozen,
twenty. He decided to try the ignition. A
whirring, growing fainter. Then dying.
Silence – except for the clatter of blades.
He tried again. He would not

droop , he would not surrender. That was not
the code of the Clarkes. The motor
would not respond. As the warriors drew
closer, he could distinguish their wild
eyes, their

droop•y hair in fierce braids. He rolled up the
windows all the way. He was feeling
calm, feeling his pulse in his temples
and chest. He'd show them. They surrounded the car. How many could he

drop before a battle-axe split his skull in half?

The city street was darker than Smith liked. As he walked, he noticed that the nearest streetlight was not working, which partly explained his feeling of

ill-bod•ing

. But not entirely, for some reason. He pulled his tweed jacket tighter and hurried down the block. Where the hell were the other people? Abruptly, from out of the darkness, an

ill-bred

person appeared, approaching in an ungainly rush from the opposite corner. They nearly collided. "Rather

ill-con•sid•ered

of you, stumbling blindly about like that," said Smith. All at once, the broken streetlight seemed to unbreak itself, and the

ill-de•fined

figure in front of him took form. About his own age, similar dark hair. Even wearing a tweed jacket, but not nearly a stylish. "You should talk," said the other man, "staggering like an

ill-dis•posed

thug – and in this unnatural darkness!" "Well," replied Smith with a sardonic smile, "*there* we agree! It should be

il•le•gal

to have these streetlights in such a crummy condition! Off, on, blinking . . . don't we citizens have a right to decent illumination?" The stranger laughed. "And half the time, the street signs are

il•leg•i•ble   !" said the man. "I hardly knew where
I was. The way the laws and statutes of
this city are made and enforced seems
like damn

il•le•git•i•ma•cy   , and I don't care who hears me," he
said. Smith, surprised, leaned forward to
look more closely at the man. Smith's
wife was certainly tired of hearing him
make similar comments about

il•le•git•i•mate   creation and enforcement of laws, while
administrators neglected their true duties.
Perhaps this guy wasn't the ruffian he
had imagined. "Yes, sometimes it seems
City Hall is more a house of

ill fame   or an insane asylum than a place that
respects the rights and furthers the goals
of its citizens!" said Smith. "I was wor-
ried our . . . meeting, you could call it,
would turn out to be

ill-fat•ed   , but we may be kindred spirits. Name's
Smith." "Well, what do you know!" said
the stranger. "I'm Smyth – you know,
with a 'y' instead of an 'i.' Less boring, I
always say. Perhaps even less

ill-fa•vored   , given how many Smiths turn up in the
news in bad ways. Not to mention some
crazy Smiths in history." "Now that's
just plain

ill-found•ed   , my friend," replied Smith. "There are
plenty of famous Smiths who performed
great deeds." "Yeah, and what about
Stan Smith and all his bloody,

ill-got•ten	gains?" "Who, the tennis pro?" "No, the Australian who was linked to 25 shootings and 15 murders." "Well, if you're going to dig up stupid things like that!" responded Smith, trying to keep
ill humor	away. He remembered a bit of trivia, but should he say it? He paused. He said it: "There's Brendan Smyth, a former monk, considered Ireland's most infamous sexual predator." "A very
il•lib•er•al	comment, as if that son of a bitch represents the entire Smyth family – or an entire nation." The streetlight flickered again, and deep down Smith wondered whether this wrong-headed stranger had any
il•lic•it	intentions. Would the next pedestrian on the block stumble upon Smith's bloody corpse? "Your kind make me sick! There was one time Jeanie and I were climbing
Il•li•ma•ni	when we bumped into –" "Wait a sec," interrupted Smith. "You climbed Illimani? In Bolivia?" "Last time I looked, that's where it was," came the response. "Fresh air, a nearly
il•lim•it•a•ble	view, no stupid Americans around . . ." Smyth stared at him with a sneer. Smith didn't know what to say. "So . . . you've climbed it, too?" "That's right. I think we had batteries powered by
il•lin•i•um	or whatever it's called these days." "And who's this Jeanie you mentioned?"

149

"What's it to you?" "That's my wife's name – and she was with me on Illimani." "Oh, go on! And she's from

Il•li•nois

, I suppose you're going to tell me next?" Smith felt a chill go down his back. "She *is* from Illinois. . . . Don't tell me *your* wife is from there as well." Smyth stared. "That visit, our assets were

il•liq•uid

, to put it in genteel terms, and we couldn't use our credit cards," said Smyth. "Nearly had to sleep in the gutter in La Paz, all sweaty and dirty. Felt like I had

il•lite

in my underwear, nearly drove me crazy." Smith's mouth was gaping as he listened. "But this . . . this story is preposterous! I can't . . . It's . . . I'm . . ." "I'll try to overlook your pathetic

il•lit•er•a•cy

, but I hope you're not suggesting that I'm a liar!" said Smyth. "The same thing happened to us," Smith replied, shaking his head. "It's like you're a kind of double of me. If you weren't so

il•lit•er•ate

, I'd even say a doppelgänger." Smyth laughed bitterly. "Yeah, right, that makes sense! But you've got it ass backwards – you must be *my* doppelgänger – and a damn

ill-look•ing

one at that!" They both flinched as the streetlight sputtered, but it stayed on. "Well, I could say some nasty things about looks – like that very old-fashioned tweed jacket – but I'm not so

ill-man•nered	," said Smith. "You should talk," responded the other man. "And I'm sure my doppelgänger, if there is such a thing, would not have the kind of
ill nature	you've demonstrated this whole time." "Wait," said Smith, "let's get this straight. Is your name William?" Smyth recoiled and his legs seemed to shake, a if suddenly struck by an
ill•ness	that threatened his equilibrium. "Who told you?" he stammered. "Who *are* you?" He stepped closer, but Smith took a step back at the same time. "This is either a scam – or there's a kind of
il•log•ic	here! You seem to know a lot about me, but it makes no sense that you would be my double. You look like something the cat dragged in – " "Now that's simply
il•log•i•cal	, Mr. So-called Smyth, with a y!" shouted Smith. "How the hell would a cat be able to drag a full-grown man in, wherever that *in* is supposed to be?" Smyth ignored him. Instead: "This detour was
ill-o•mened	, that's for sure! Meeting a psychopath in a dark alley – and where *is* everyone? Is this a city or what?" "That's what I'm wondering," said Smith, peeking over his shoulder. "We're very
ill-sort•ed	to be doubles – a rather boorish type like you and a well-dressed, articulate gentleman like me! Don't match up at all." "If that's what you call articulate, your days in school were obviously

ill-spent	," said Smyth. "You're a walking cliché." He took another step forward, and again Smith stepped back. "This whole visit to the city was
ill-starred	, meeting a crazy loser like you!" he said. "I suppose you never finished high school." "College, magna cum laude," retorted the other. "Whoa, same here," said Smith. He was feeling
ill-suit•ed	for a struggle on this shadowy block. Didn't a doppelgänger sometimes try to kill the other person? He made fists and raised them protectively. And this guy is certainly the
ill-tem•pered	sort. "What's your favorite color?" Smyth suddenly asked. "Huh?" "You heard me." "Blue," replied Smith. "No!" "Followed by green – and I hate pink." "No way!" Smith's bold step ahead was
ill-timed	, because Smyth was moving as well. They nearly collided, then sprang back, cursing. And the curses were very similar – involving God, hell, and several adverbs, as well as a threat to
ill-treat	the other's "hairy backside." Then came a woman's voice: "Bill?" Smith turned, just as another voice came from the other end: "Bill?" They froze, stared at each other – then ran in opposite directions.

152

verminous — vernal

E-MAIL #1 (March 2): Ah, to be free at last of the

ver•min•ous

city, its squalor, its noise, its hair-trigger people! How weary we were of overrated hot spots like Chez Veronique, witless society people like Jake and Muffy!

Ver•mont

, in contrast, is true peace. Breezes whisper, trees sigh, and as Ellen mixes the gin and

ver•mouth

, I gaze off the snowy hillside into the calm of evening. And, oh! these quaint villagers with their

ver•nac•u•lar

charm!
E-MAIL #2 (March 16): God, the quiet is maddening! And the view, the goddamn view puts me to sleep. How we miss the fresh bagels! The unchanging

ver•nac•u•lar•ism

of these yokels – it's like crickets chirping, chirping, chirping! The same damn one-word answers, the tug at the forelock! Please, Jerry, rescue us before the deadly

ver•nal

thaw floods the back roads and traps us here! We need you! Action! Taxis honking! An insult in Spanish or Yiddish! Even a cockroach would entertain us. Help

accompanist — accordion

The celebrated diva Signorina Brunetti, the Italian Nightingale, and Vanessa Pym, her faithful

ac•com•panist , stood at the railing as the liner slowly pulled away from yet another foreign harbor. It was known among a certain substratum of humanity that La Signorina preferred her jewels to

ac•com•pa•ny her on every voyage. Which was the reason for the discreet presence, on board, of Maxie the Dip and his faithful

ac•com•plice , Stuart Manchester. "So how ya propose to

ac•com•plish the heist, Maxie?" "Shhh! You want people should hear you?" Sometimes he wondered how he'd ever

ac•com•plished anything with a nitwit like Stuart, whose main

ac•com•plish•ment was a gleaming smile for the ladies and an air of elegance. "Zip it! Here they come." As they drew near, the diva was telling Miss Pym, "*Bene*! So we are in

ac•cord , Meez Pym? Do not let eet out of your sight. Remove yourself to zee cabin *immediatamente*!" This could be their big chance, thought Maxie. So, in

ac•cord•ance with their plans, they hurried below to observe what Miss Pym would do. Unconcerned, she entered the cabin and let the door close slowly behind her. But it was an

ac•cord•ant

note Fate had struck, for the lock did not catch. In a moment, the men had slipped inside. There sat Miss Pym, patting the top of a large, square case. "Good grief, Stu –

ac•cord•ing

to the size of that thing, it's gotta hold a king's ransom in jewels!" Pushing Miss Pym aside, they grabbed the case and acted

ac•cord•ing•ly

– beat it to the life boats and swiped one. If they could reach the harbor before the police mobilized. . . . "Got it!" muttered Maxie, as the lock gave. There, nestled on velvet, was Miss Pym's

ac•cor•di•on

, loyal companion of many successful tours. Wailing and moaning – unmusically – they hardly noticed that the police patrol boat was fast approaching.

Lisle —— literati

"What's all this – " "Name, please."
"Not until I know what's going on here.
I demand – " "Name, please." "Jared

Lisle
." "Thank you. That's what we suspected.
Is that L-Y-L-E?" "No, it's L-I-S-L-E.
The 's' is silent." "Foreign name, then?
We should have guessed." "What does
that mean? Haven't you heard of

lisle
, the cotton thread? That's not foreign!
And what if it was?" "Yes, what if it
was." "What does *that* mean? Are you
insinuating something? And you still
haven't told me – " "Please try not to

lisp
, Mr. Lis-lee. It will make this whole
procedure much more difficult." "I
wasn't lisping!" "So you have something against people who lisp? Consider
them inferior to you? Well, that's

lis pen•dens
, something to investigate at another
time. We have more important concerns
at present." "And the first of them is
telling me what the hell is going on!
Why am I here?" "What about your

lis•some
companion? Forget all about her already?"
"Joan? Of course not, but you let her
go . . . didn't you?" "Perhaps. In some
important way, that's not our concern.
It's the

list
that we are concerned with here. Con-

156

centrate on that." "Which

list
? I don't know what you're talking about. My goddamn grocery

list
? Did you want to check whether I was planning to buy skim milk or cream? . . Or some arsenic?" "Arsenic. Now why would you say that, Mr. Lis-lee." "I was exaggerating. What's on *your*

list
?" "We ask the questions here, Mr. Lis-lee. You are an architect?" "Yes, not that it's any of your business." "What's a

list•el
?" "It's a narrow molding." "Exactly. But that could have been a lucky guess." "Whatever. You still haven't told me what I'm doing here – or who the hell you are to be holding me." "You don't

lis•ten
very well, do you, Mr. Lis-lee. I've already told you it's about the list." "Which list?" "That's what we're trying to establish. What if I said that you are on the list?" "And this list is derived from a

lis•ten•ing post
near the Chinese embassy or a scrap of paper found on the subway?" "Very funny, Mr. Lis-lee, but I can assure you this is not a laughing matter. Just who the

list•er
is is our business, not yours. The fact that your name appears there is your concern and ours." "So, Jared Lisle or this Lis-lee person you keep addressing? Make up your mind." "At this point, the

list•er is less important than the listee – *you*, in other words." "How very flattering. But you don't even know who I am, or even how to pronounce my name." "So you believe." "I'm thinking it's Joseph

Lis•ter you're after, how about that?" "Who?" "The father of antiseptic surgery." "Quite droll, Mr. Lis-lee. First you mention arsenic, then a field with rather dangerous instruments. Interesting." "Are you

list•ing all these interesting little things I'm saying?" "Well, what do you think, Mr. Lis-lee? Do you think we'd bring you in here just to pass the time?" "To be frank, when it comes to your habits, I'm

list•less — or, to clarify, I don't give a damn. What I give a damn about is why I'm here." "That's understandable. . . . The watch you are wearing, it looks expensive. What was the

list price ?" "I don't remember. Also, it's none of your business." "That's where you're wrong." "Look, mister, you can take your

lists and stick them up your ass. I demand to call my lawyer." "As it turns out, we tried to reach him earlier. Got put on hold and had to listen to some boring

Liszt until we hung up. He's probably on the ski slopes. Our people also stopped by your place. Pretty

lit up, but nobody else seemed around."

"Who the hell do you think you are, prowling around people's homes?" "The people whose job it is to prowl around people's homes. We noticed you have half a

lit. of milk left in the refrigerator, some sliced turkey that seems close to going bad. Also, you – or someone else – left a book by a

Li Tai Po on the kitchen table. Who's that, one of your foreign authors? Can't find any Americans worthy of your dollar, Mr. Lis-lee?" "One of the T'ang poets." "Fine. I don't want to hear a

lit•a•ny about your exotic tastes . . . unless, that is, they have some bearing on the list." "Speaking of boring litanies, you've got a good one going here, mister. Sounds like you're a real

Lit.B. " "Meaning what?" "Bachelor of Litanies. Or Literate Bullshitter. Take your pick." "Thank you, Mr. Lis-lee. Tell me, have you ever eaten a

li•tchi nut? I ask because of your xanthous reading habits. . . . And didn't you mention the Chinese embassy earlier? We'll have the transcript, of course. Maybe you had a few bottles of Tsingtao

-lite in your refrigerator that we didn't notice the first time, hidden from sight behind your

li•ter of milk." "Your lists sound endlessly fascinating. How lucky you must be to be able to live such full, interesting lives. And I'm pleasantly surprised that

lit•er•a•cy actually seems to be one of the qualities your employers look for when they hire. Will there be a

lit•er•al transcript of everything we've said here this evening? Or just the highlights?" "Very amusing, Mr. Lis-lee. But perhaps you'll change your mind on the value of

lit•er•al•ism when we confront you with the list. I suspect you won't be able to wiggle out of things so handily." "Do you mean *wriggle*?" "Ah! There you have us again but, let me stress, we prize

lit•er•al•i•ty . Words can be so weasely, don't you agree?" "I couldn't agree more. So please show me the list, so we can

lit•er•al•ize and actualize the document. Then perhaps I can answer some of your concerns – if they really exist." "If only we could, Mr. Lis-lee! But you are not permitted to see the list. There are

lit•er•al•ly only a handful of people with sufficient clearance to see that list – or in fact any of our lists. These are not mere

lit•er•ar•y productions, you see. They're governmental matters of extremely high sensitivity." "Well done! I think it's quite likely that you've passed the test." "What test, Mr.

Lis-lee?" "You've proven

lit•er•ate

and efficient. I think we can remove you
from our list." "What list? *I'm* the one
with the list." "Yes, isn't it pretty to
think so." "You're bluffing." "You'd
think that. But once I rejoin the

lit•er•a•ti

with our Li Tai Po and our endless
lists, we'll consider how you fared to
day." "It won't work, Mr. Lis-lee."
"That's not even my name." "You . . .
it's quite impossible. . . . I . . ."

The way I heard it, once in an offseason exhibition at the Stadium, Biff O'Day, the Baron of Boom, put on a particularly

fear•some show, rocketing balls clear out of the park. Soon a guy shows up near home plate: "Knock it off, Mr. O. You've done a

fea•sance of injury to personal property — one of your swats broke our window, landed in the slicer, and the whole machine is *farchadat*." "Ain't

fea•si•ble . Them balls are goin' out west, but your deli's on the east side of the avenue," says the Baron, who'd been known to

feast on pastrami on pumpernickel or corned beef on rye at the shop after a game. "Ah, I'd show you a thing or two about hitting if we weren't getting ready for the

Feast of Lots , Mister Big Shot." So O'Day flips him the bat. The deli-man hefts it. First pitch: smash over the wall. Second pitch: same place. "Nice

feat of hitting, Joe," says the Baron. "Name's Herschel," replies the man. "But you can call me the Rebbe of Ribbies." For his next

feat , Herschel smacks a high drive, then launches the next pitch right after it. PLOK! The second ball knocks the first

clear into the seats. "Not bad," grunts
O'Day. So then the Baron, swinging only a

feath•er plucked from one of those damn stadium
pigeons, powers the next pitch into the
upper deck. "You win," says the deli
-man. "Post-workout snack's on us!"

Jenkins had no doubt that his distinguished forebears would be

a•ghast at his present line of work. But in this day and age, when jobs were few and the family fortunes were otherwise deployed, one had to be

ag•ile , willing to experiment, willing to take risks. He was profoundly weary of hearing how Ancestor This had fought in the Crusades or Ancestor That had been at

Ag•in•court . "Doing what?" he had once asked Sir Frederick. "Robbing the corpses of the arrow-riddled Frenchies?" That had cost him some invitations to dinner. Later, his great-aunt had suggested he try

ag•i•o , as she had delicately called it, hoping that the archaic name would soften the stigma of being a money-grubbing businessman. "Oh, yes, I dabble in currency exchange, a spot of

ag•i•o•tage now and then, when I can drag myself from the family estate to London." No, not his cup of tea. His opinions on the *ancien régime* were known to

ag•i•tate the family, so much so that his uncle, defending his long tenure at Lloyd's – or was it Barclay's? – once became so

ag•i•tat•ed that he dropped a lighted pipe into his

lap and nearly burned down the mansion. An exaggeration, that – but the pompous ass swore Jenkins would someday come crawling back. But might a bit of

ag•i•ta•tion be good for an ossified heart – or a numb brain? "So what do you actually *do*?" asked Dorothea. "How on earth, I might add, did you get tickets for this concert?" Jenkins waited until the

a•gi•ta•to segment of the determinedly avant-garde music ended. "Oh, I have my ways." "Bosh!" put in Reggie. "You're a union

ag•i•ta•tor , secretly working for the authorities to wreak havoc." "Oh, if only it were so noble!" replied Jenkins. "I'd still be in my family's good graces." "I have it — you produce

ag•it•prop for the anti-immigration movement!" said Dorothea. "Alas, no. Do you see Lady Frances, three rows ahead of us? I was hired by her randy husband to take certain photographs. . . . She became

A•gla•ia , goddess of beauty. You have my word that, with her hair undone, sprawled on the Persian rug, naked and oiled flesh

a•gleam , you would barely recognize her. . . . Ah, and there's another respectable wife who would much prefer not to see me. Excuse me while I bury my face in the programme."

Namaqualand — Namibia

"Hey, who's the doofus at Miller's old desk? He's dressed like he got his clothes at a fire sale in

Na•ma•qua•land or something. Looks like he's still wet behind the ears. Well, if he expects me to give him a big salaam or

na•mast•e , he's painfully mistaken. Joe McCoy worked his way up the hard way at Santini, Inc., and he's not kissing the derriere of some new

nam•by-pam•by junior executive. Say, what's the bozo's

name ?" "Look, Joe, I don't see why you have to go

name-calling like that. He's just a little inexperienced, that's all." "Yeah, sure — and I suppose he expects a big shiny apple on his

name day , like all the other sad excuses for managers Old Man Santini has hired over the years. Hear that? The little

name-drop•per just mentioned our retired senior v.p., like they're chums or something. Yeah, right. Like this

name•less twerp knows the honchos of the company already! Well, Joe McCoy is gonna put him in his place —

name•ly , by letting him know what's what in this

office. . . . Say, buddy. Yeah, you — the new guy with the big sparkling

name•plate   on Miller's old desk. Joe McCoy here. Listen, I got a few things to explain to you, stuff you'd better damn well learn. What's the moniker?" "It's Philip Santini." "Hey, you're the

name•sake   of the Big Guy! What a hoot! I mean, what're the odds . . . I mean . . . Uh, well." "Ah, so glad you stopped by, Mr. McCoy. Now I can inform you that your new assignment will be in

Na•mib•i•a   . Hope you enjoy your stay."

"She's just the right sort to tutor me on my French pronunciation. A most unpretentious,

un•de•sign•ing

, unspoiled young woman," said Senator Higginson, wiping his brow. "You think so?" asked Miss Towers dubiously. "Oh, I grant you, she's not

un•de•sir•a•ble

, if one's thoughts were inclined that way," said the senator quickly. "But there's no time to waste. Please send her in." Minutes later, Mademoiselle Brie entered,

un•did

the top button of her blouse, and patted her neck with a scented hankie. "*Mon Dieu*, eet eez very 'ot! Even my — 'ow you say? —

un•dies

weel be drenched!" To distract himself, the senator glanced down at her feet, shod in cheap rubber flip flops. "Miss Brie, I have a session with the press shortly." Oh, she was a veritable

un•dine

, he thought, imagining her prancing through the waves at Cannes. Perhaps this was not such a wise decision. But if he gave his speech in Paris totally

un•di•rect•ed

, he would look like a fool. "Bahn joor?" "Oh, no, Senator," she laughed. "You say 'bone zhoor,' you understand?" "Joor?" "Oh, you Americans are so

un•dis•posed	to exercise your cheeks and leeps in the propair manner!" she exclaimed. Think, *think* about
un•dis•so•ci•a•ted	molecules, he told himself — or currency exchange. "Now *you* say, Senator. *'Bon jour, mesdames et messieurs.'* Oh, so 'ot eet eez!" And she began to
un•do	her second and then third buttons. Yes, his advisors had warned that this Paris speech could be his
un•do•ing	! "Permit me," he panted, fingers fumbling until her blouse was completely
un•done	. "Oh, Monsieur! Your touch eez . . . so gentle." In bustled Miss Towers with the photographers: "Senator, the press is here to . . . *Senator*!" "Hell, I'm
un•done	! Kaput!" The flashbulbs dazzled. *"Fini,* you mean?" queried Mademoiselle Brie

Zephyrus — Zeus

Zeph•y•rus

zep•pe•lin

ze•ro

zero gravity

zero hour

ze•ro-ze•ro

zest

ze•ta

Zet•land

"Yes, we have a difficult road ahead," said the captain. "Even

himself seems against us, sending his wind to rebuff our advance." And sure enough, the

was slowing down in the face of the wind. Lieutenant Stoessel stared gloomily ahead: "Our chances are

! We're doomed!" "Calm yourself," replied the captain. "One would think that the enjoyable experience of

itself would captivate you." "What do I care for such things now, as

fast approaches? I have a sweetheart back in Dusseldorf!" "Captain," called one of the crew, "the timer has nearly reached

. Shall I give her more power?" "Very well, Mueller," replied the captain with such evident

that his second-in-command could only shake his head. "The code name for this operation, as you know, is

, representing our destination,

— or, as the natives seem to prefer, Shetland. We require silence and stealth, as well as the sheer courage to do what must be done should we be discovered. Now! Recall that

zeug•ma , our motto: *Advance filled with helium — as well as hope!*" "And if the Scots shoot us down for spying on their national soccer team in training?" howled Stoessel. Replied the captain, "Then not even

Zeus Himself can help us, I'm afraid."

Pushtu — puss

MEN! ARE YOU A WEAKLING? So what if you speak Portuguese or

Push•tu   , or know all the capitals of Africa, or can explain relativity? What you really need is a regimen of

push-up   , roadwork, and punching-bag. Don't let those

push•y   morons walk all over you. Do you want Irma to think that you're a

pu•sil•lan•i•mous   pipsqueak? NO! Clip this coupon NOW! And next time they come around bothering you and your pretty little

puss   , show her — and them — who's boss! Bop 'em on the brow! Toss 'em on their tushy! ACT TODAY!

macumba —— madhouse

ma•cum•ba

"Um, are you feeling all right, Madeline?" he asks me. If he only knew! If it all goes well, it will be like something out o

. Entice him into a dance, lean close, whisper hot nonsense into his ear, let him inhale this magical perfume — that will drive him

mad

with desire. That, at least, is what was told me in the dark backstreets of that seaport in

Mad•a•gas•car

, where everyone murmured the praises of

mad•am

Zora, the love-witch. She, they told me, would know the secrets. So I went to her. "Tell me,

mad•ame

, how can I make my man want me until his body is on fire? For he is never one for

mad•cap

antics. His work is too much with him." "And shall I give you the secret to

mad•den

him, pale woman?" she asked me. "The passion perfume?" "Yes!" I said. "Yes!" And now we dance. I slide and slither. He shudders. His expression is hard to read. Is he

mad•der

already? "Henry," I whisper. "Sorry, hon. Seem to have an ant down the back of my shirt." "But are you mad with desire, Henry?" "Sure, babycakes, but I'd b

173

mad•der   if the bank refuses to cash our American Express tomorrow morning." So I go, "Let's samba over to the shadows there, away from this

mad•ding   crowd, if you don't mind." He stares about him, tilting his head critically. "Well, not madding, perhaps;

mad•dish   is how I'd put it." "Henry! Dance with me! The night is simply

made   for love." "Actually, studies have shown that . . ." "Oh, shut up and have some of this intoxicating

Ma•deir•a   , and then tell me how much you want to tear my clothing off me!" "Sure, my scrumptious little

mad•e•leine   , but won't that be awfully expensive? It's not like you can just prance into a department store in this neck of the woods and find another dress." "Henry?" "Yes,

Mad•e•line   ?" "Forget all that. Tonight you are a sailor, just back from a voyage to Tortuga or Baffin Island in your yawl, and you spot me, under a street light, a

ma•de•moi•selle   who seems none too innocent — and hungry!" "Well, then, let's see if there's a table at Señor

Ma•de•ro   's restaurant." "Henry, Henry! That's not what I meant! The music, the sensual night breeze, my perfumed shoulders —

174

are they not

made-to-or•der

for you, Sergio, the prowling sailor,
famished for some —" "Well, as I pointed
out, there's Señor —" "Oh, Henry! Listen!
See what's before you! She — that is,
I — like a

made-up

tart, willing to meet your every fantasy.
Yes, Sergio, take me now!" He blinks.
"Um, so you're someone else?" "Yes!
Call me Leda, or la Principessa d'Amor
. . ." "Or

Madge

?" "Madge? Who's Madge?" I seize
him. "Oh, it's just a name." "Just a name,
eh? Why did that particular name come
to you? Oh, Henry, you'll send me to the

mad•house

if you keep this up!" But now his eyes
smolder! He bruises my lips with his.
"Madge, Madge!" Madge? Well, different
strokes, I suppose, sighing under one of his

"I'm afraid it's totally out of the question. You can't see the

vice•roy this evening. He's entertaining the Comte de Montignac and Minister Kreutzer of the German Navy and not to be disturbed." "Look, I don't care if he's entertaining the

vice•roy•al•ty of Beelzebub and Belial. He's going to see me, and pronto!" "Very well. Whom shall I say is calling?" "This whom happens to be Inspector Maggio of the

vice squad , got that?" A few minutes later: "Yes, Smithers? . . . Well, tell him to . . . ah, I see I shall be able to tell him myself. How delightful to see you again, Inspector Maggio." "Yeah, and

vi•ce ver•sa , I'm sure." "To what do I owe this pleasure? Haven't I answered all your questions about the missing schoolgirl?" "We've turned up a witness who'd been an . . . associate of yours in

Vi•chy , helping to move . . . merchandise. A certain Raoul. Ring a bell, Your Excellency?" "Preposterous, Maggio. I demand to call my lawyer." "Very good idea. And you know what? This

vi•chy•ssoise you have the temerity to serve has way too much salt."

dread — dredge

Marlowe straightened his collar with his callused hands. Then he passed into the twilight of the bar, fighting his

dread

. Some of them, he saw, were there. Which was worse – to be ignored, or to be noticed? He soon had his answer. "It's simply

dread·ful

who wanders into this place. There's Marlowe, that clumsy airhead from high school." "I'm

dread·ful·ly

sorry, I beg your pardon." Stumbling over someone's feet, he walked to a stool near the end of the bar and sat down. There, on the coaster, was a fine rendering of a

dread·nought

, Royal Navy, circa 1908. No doubt designed by Carruthers. It was cutting through the waves like a

dream

, its fierce guns glittering. "Lieutenant Marlowe, reporting for duty, sir!" Then he heard the young women, two stools away, laughing. "That Chuck is a real

dream·boat

, isn't he! Handsome, with a good head on his shoulders. He's making good money in his father's company, not like some hangdog

dream·er

who doesn't know which way is up." Marlowe recognized her voice. Maura.

And with her, Sheryl. "What'll it be, chief?" "Bass Ale, please." Maybe that would bring him a taste of

dream·land , where the haughty ocean would dash against the cliffs, but Marlowe and his battleship still cruised out imperiously to confront Kreutzer's fleet. "And you know Chuck never gets lost in a

dream world like some people we know," Sheryl was saying. "Hush, look at that guy next to You Know Who! He's

dream·y !" "No kidding! I wouldn't mind sailing to Tortuga on *his* boat." Marlowe's ale tasted good, but it could not keep a

drear mood from weighing upon him. He drained his glass and set it on the coaster, obscuring the ship.

The next morning was wet and

drear·y as he strode alongside the channel. He unlocked the door and turned on the machinery. There was a rumble that shook the cabin. He lowered the protesting shovel of the

dredge into the channel, scooping the mud and slime. No time to waste on silly dreams. No time at all.

"So, where will we go this year? Paris, London, Rome?" "Oh, honey, you know we can't afford those – not with the kids too." "How about the

Vaal   River, in South Africa? Or . . . wait! This sounds like a great deal, in some place 'off the beaten track.' Well, at these prices . . ." It was two months later when Gene removed the "no

va·can·cy   " sign from the boarded window of the rough-hewn wood cabin in rural Pennsylvania. "Gee, Dad, no wonder it was

va·cant   , in the middle of nowhere like this!" said Timmy. "Little Brother is right, for once," piped up Janie. "I'd like to

va·cate   the premises, as they say in the cop shows, right now. It's too quiet and spooky!" "Oh, children, you've been watching too many bad movies," said Eileen. "Why don't we just try to enjoy our

va·ca·tion   and make the best of things? It's hard enough getting your father to be a

va·ca·tion·er   at all, with his hectic work schedule." "All right, Mom," said Timmy with a cute little pout. "But this sure don't look like no

va·ca·tion·land   !" "Timmy, watch the language, please," said Gene. "We don't want you sounding like some illiterate street gangster." As Eileen unpacked her underwear, she again wondered about matters

vac·ci·nal . She'd wanted to have everything as safe as can be, but Gene insisted it was wrong to

vac·ci·nate willy-nilly. "Although there are so many dread diseases that it can prevent,

vac·ci·na·tion is not risk-free. Why don't we lay off until we have a better sense of what's threatening out there – and then see if there's a specific

vac·cine that will help." "Well, there's always avian flu or bubonic plague or even

vac·cin·i·a , which is not something I'd care to catch!" But Gene, imagining himself as *pater familias*, tried not to waver. "But what about Lyme disease?" asked Janie. Gene seemed a little

vac·il·lant on that score, hemming and hawing as he pondered. "Especially with wild deer running around." "And the grass is kinda yellow," added Timmy. "We might catch yellow fever." Try not to

vac·il·late , Gene told himself, tugging on his collar. *Cholera*! Could this out-of-the-way place be especially vulnerable to that horrid disease? As he continued

vac·il·lat·ing , a strange blue mist enveloped the cabin and the surrounding terrain. "Cool color," said Timmy. "Try not to breathe it in, dear," said Eileen. They woke the next morning to a shout: "It's the

vac·u·a

plague! Get out before it's too late!" When Gene opened the door, broom held as a weapon, a wild-eyed stranger stood on the porch. "What's the vacua plague?" Gene asked. "It's the coming o

va·cu·ity

! It turns everything into a vacuum of one sort or another, working through your body and into your mind." He paused for breath. "Name's Burt, but most call me Mysterious Old Man. It's

vac·u·o·late

sort of plague, starting in your teeny, tiny vacuoles, which are membrane-bound compartments in some eukaryotic cells." "Heck," said Timmy, "what's that?" "Don't know, but if a body'

vac·u·o·la·tion

is correct, they seem to serve a bunch o secretory, excretory, and storage function: And" – he lowered his voice – "folks say they may be involved in . . . autoph agy." Eileen gasped. "Was that a

vac·u·ole

by that tree over there? If we'd been vaccinated yesterday, none of this would've happened!" "Lady, I ain't sur there's a vaccine against the vacua plague." "Mom, I'm feeling . . . a bit . .

vac·u·ous

," said Janie, patting her forehead. "Who's Paris Hilton going out with these days?" "Oh, Janie! It's . . . it's started," said Eileen, hugging her. "What's J.Lo's favorite perfume? . . . Oh, now the

vac·u·um	's got me, too!" "Sit down, hon," ordered Gene. "Let me get you some nice, cold water from the bottle over there." But when he drew closer, he saw that it had mutated into a
vacuum bottle	! Aghast, he threw up on the floor, soiling the hem of his pants. "Quick, get me the spray cleaner before this vomit sinks in!" Eileen dashed to the sink. But the cleaner, she saw, was now a
vacuum cleaner	, and she covered her eyes. "It's . . . it's changed horribly!" "This is serious, folks," said Burt. "Never seen it quite this bad, so quickly. You'd best get you one of them doohickeys, a
vacuum gauge	, so you know when household objects are near about to mutate. . . . The general store has 'em at a good price." "What did Justin say to Rosie that got Kanye so upset?" said Gene. "Hell, I'm
vacuum-packed	with brain-destroying trivia! . . . If we leave now, right now, maybe we'll be saved." "Yes!" shouted Timmy, with a
vacuum pump	of the fist. "Oops." "Into the car!" said Gene. "And we'll figure what's worse – having static cling or the wrong shade of lipstick." At the door, Janie shrieked. Her tube top had turned into a
vacuum tube	top, and her modest-sized breasts had vanished entirely! "Oh, Mom, no boys will like me now!" Watching the car roar away, Burt wondered whether they'd get any of their deposit back.

Hindustan — hip

Old Fart: "I always say, when in Rome, do as the Romans." Young Turk: "And, no doubt, when in

Hin•du•stan

, one should become as much a

Hin•du•sta•ni

as possible?" Old Fart: "No doubt, no doubt." The ashes of his smoldering cigar dropped unnoticed into his lap. "Believe me, the entire success of a diplomatic career can

hinge

upon such fine points. One must know a hawk from a handsaw." Young Turk: "And no doubt a

hinge joint

from a

hin•ny

?" Old Fart: "Indubitably." He coughed for several seconds. "Remember, while representing your country, you are woo- ing the other nation! If a Foreign Servic codger can drop a

hint

," he said, leaning over and exuding an odor of tobacco and mildew, "you are the seducer. Oh, one can be oneself, as it were in a cosmopolitan capital, but out in the

hin•ter•land

, things may be very different. Why, as a young man, I was not, as you fellows today put it, very

hip

, and when a native hostess once spilled some foul concoction on my left

hip   as I sat at the banquet table, I thought I was meant to reciprocate. War, I must say, loomed on the horizon. Thank God Bertie, the British ambassador, stepped in." Young Turk: "Let's have a

hip   ,

hip   , hurray for the Union Jack, shall we?"

Jocelin — joggle

Her name sounded somewhat English to me, the kind of name the daughter of a stuffy baronet would have:

Joc·e·lin

. Or maybe even the stuffy baronet himself. You never knew with the English. She seemed to be something of a

jock

, striding about the campus with a knapsack hanging down her back and the handle of a squash racquet poking out like an ensign. As slender as a

jock·ey

, she still drew the attention of many of the fraternity guys whose houses bounded the main campus walkway. They had the manners of a pet

jock·o

grabbing for peanuts. This afternoon, Hank waved from his doorway, wearing cut-off jeans and flip flops, with a

jock·strap

on his head. "Hey, sugar pie! What's the hurry? Give us a kiss!" And his

jo·cose

companion, Dooley, held on to a column for support and made kissing noises. "You weren't so cold last weekend, were you, babe?" Their

jo·cos·i·ty

entertained them mightily and they burst out in raucous laughter. "Well, if it isn't the

joc·u·lar

jerks, squirming with jock itch," she

said, halting a moment on the walk. "Can't find any woman stupid enough to give you the time of day?" "Oh, Jossie dear, you weren't so

joc·und last weekend when that greasy freshman from Banjermasin or

Jodh·pur was trotting around behind you like a whipped dog." "Yeah, Little Miss Snobby," added Dooley. "The sucker seemed to think he had a chance to get into your

jodh·pur . Did you let him?" "And you should hear what Randy and

Joe are saying about that little purchase you made at the drug store. Did it come out the right color?" At which point, I came down from the porch across the walk. "Care for some

joe at the coffee shop, Jocelin? It can't be fun listening to these two morons soil themselves." "Well, well, look who it is –

Joe College himself, with the big books and the big vocabulary." "Yeah, but I bet I know one thing of his that isn't big!" said Hank with another laugh. I wished I could hurl back the burning words of

Jo·el or Amos or Jeremiah, but all I did was look at her. "The Coffee shop! Yeah, go there for a latte and a side dish of

joe-pye weed and watercress, that's your style," shouted Dooley, hopping on his porch like an overeager

jo·ey   . "Well," said Jocelin, nodding, "we should take a lesson from General

Jof·fre   and know when it's time to retreat." She took my arm and we walked to the next corner. And around it. And once out of their line of vision, she released me and began to

jog   ahead. "Thanks, Sam," she called over her shoulder. "Sorry you had to get involved." I knew what I wanted to say. But all I said was, "No problem." And I stood there and watched her

jog   up the sidewalk, watched the handle of her racquet bob, until she was nearly out of sight. Mister Tongue-Tied. I gave my head a

jog·gle   , praying that something eloquent would come to mind. And then she was gone, again.

187

"Well, let's see how it goes with Judge I'm-the-Star. . . . Ladies and gentlemen of the jury, my client is accused of assault with a deadly weapon – a palpably ludicrous charge! A

quoit , last time I looked, is not a weapon. It is part of a harmless game. So we must ask,

quo ju·re? — by what right has Mr. Black, the assistant district attorney, brought such a case? It must be mentioned that he has some well-established ties with the supposed victim. Again, we must ask

quo mo·do ? Why does this trial proceed? It should have been tossed out from the first. Yes, remember this fact: the A.D.A. is a

quon·dam fraternity brother of Mr. Smythe . . . and those ties are lasting!" "Your Honor, does Mr. Mazzini expect me to recuse myself and spend the next two weeks in a

Quon·set hut in the wilderness?" "I'm sorry, Mr. Black – I was distracted by the flashes going off. What were you saying?" "I was suggesting that if the counselor for the defense retained a

quo·rum of his wits, he would abandon this insulting approach." "Thank you, Mr. Black. I'm running this trial, *lex fori* and *ipso jure*, and I will decide what's what.

I am reminded of a

quot.   from Oliver Wendell Holmes, in which he — " "Your Honor, surely you have already used up your

quo·ta   of illustrative anecdotes for the entire trial!" "You're out of order, Mr. Mazzini, and I must ask *quare impedit*. If there's a

quot·a·ble   anecdote or interesting bit of trivia, I believe it enriches the trial. For example, did you know that quoits was the favorite pastime of Chief Justice John Marshall? A good

quo·ta·tion   is worth . . ." "But, Your Honor, the prosecution has still not established how a quoit can be a deadly weapon." "Perhaps Mr. Mazzini, that phrase should be surrounded by a

quotation mark   on either side, indicating it's a *kind* of deadly weapon, an object not a weapon *qua* weapon in and of itself but with certain weaponly applications, *ipsissima verba*." "Your Honor, if I can

quote   an unknown philosopher, 'What the hell are you smoking?' That argument can be applied to *any* household object!" "Exactly Counselor. The home is the most dangerous place of all! Why,

quoth   Edmund in *King Lear*: 'With his preparèd sword he charges home.' I rest my case." "Your Honor, traditionally you're not the one who rests his case." "Well, Mr. Black,

quoth·a ! You got me there! But why don't you show the defense team how a quoit can be used as a weapon so we can push beyond this silly nitpicking?" "Thank you, Your Honor. This

quo·tid·i·an object, this quoit, is much more dangerous than it first appears. It's metal, for one thing. For another, although it is customarily tossed lightly, it can be hurled viciously as well. If we take the

quo·tient , i.e., the number of times a quoit is tossed divided by the number of times it has been used to intimidate or harm an opponent, we – " "Objection, Your Honor! This is gobbledygook! I demand

quo war·ran·to , to discover by which right my deranged opponent holds his office in our legal system!" "*You can't handle the truth*, eh, Counselor? Interestingly enough, even the

Qu·ran holds the legal system in high esteem. According to Shar'iah, if a man brings suit – excuse me, which profile do you prefer for the photo?" "Precisely, Your Honor. Nobody knows the value of a

qursh or a riyal better than you." "Thank you, Mr. Assistant District Attorney. And what is it *now*, Mr. Mazzini?" "I demand a mistrial, Your Honor. According to *Bishop v. Knight*,

q.v. , if undue – " "Which reminds me – and I suspect the jury will be interested, too

– Joey Bishop wasn't a real bishop, and he wasn't even Christian! Whether Bobby Knight is a knight is a

qy. that must still be answered, *coram nobis*. As for you, Mr. Mazzini: guilty, guilty, guilty! And that goes for your client as well.

"Oh, Carlo, Carlo, *vieni qui*, you old bastard!" said the don from his hospital bed. "If I still had a

smid•gen

of good sense, you'd be dead now. Cold meat! But this wreath you bring with all that nice green

smi•lax

and everything — well, I tell ya, I've just gotta

smile

. Sure, there are times in this world, being what it is, when you gotta

smirch

a guy's reputation, or go all the way with a rub-out. Yeah, you can

smirk

a little, Carlo *mio*, but you understand. Your enemy gives you trouble, you

smite

him — just like in the Bible. Am I right or am I right? Joey there, he knows, too — don't you, Joey? And regrets, bad feelings? Nah. Does a goddamn

smith

shed a tear when he hammers the steel? Do Mr.

Smith

and Mr. Wesson weep when their well-crafted tools do their task? But this is a lovely wreath, Carlo," he said, sniffing in pleasure, moments before it blew him and Joey to

smith•er•eens

. Climbing to his feet from behind the other bed, Carlo made his way down the corridor to the emergency exit. Alarms were blaring.

Quai d'Orsay — Quaker

Quai d'Or•say

quail

quail

quaint

quake

Quak•er

"Welcome, Ambassador Fenwick. I am sure you will find that we at the

are quite civilized — in our own Gallic fashion." "I never had any doubt about that, Monsieur le Ministre." "Excellent. And do you hunt, Ambassador Fenwick The

season has begun. Claudette and I woul⁃ be most honored to have you as our weekend guest at our little place in the country." "I

at the thought of shooting defenseless little birds, but I would be delighted to accept your invitation, Monsieur le Min⁃ istre." "How

! And yet you Americans think nothing of sending missiles into populated areas — for strategic advantage." "Exactly, much as many a former French colony has learned to

at the sight of your glorious paratrooper⁃ on their way to restore — how do you put it? — order? civilization?" "Ah, I see we understand each other. For us, civilization is

Oats, Perrier, McDonald's, Peugeot, IBM, Speculor, is it not?" "Still, Monsieur le Ministre, we must not overlook those things of the spirit, *n'est-ce pas?*"

It was obvious, at least to someone of Mr. Fotheringay's refined sensibility, that Miss Murgatroyd was of not

un•gen•er•ous

proportions. Even her dowdy clothes covered with chalk dust could not conceal her shapeliness. Oh, how he dreamed! If only someday he could

un•gird

his loins, and hers, perhaps even here in the Common Room, with its prim volumes of Bagehot, Fichte, and Hudson's fairy tales, when no one else was about. Then, having

un•girt

, they would steam the windows with their passion, until, their minds

un•glued

and their senses rioting, they'd cry out together in ecstasy. He sighed. She, an arm's length away, wondered again about the

un•god•ly

emotions roiling within her. It was almost as if she'd fallen under a macumba spell. Nobly, she tried to correct the student essay but suffered an almost

un•gov•ern•a•ble

urge to toss it aside, throw off her clothes, and take him in her arms — provided, of course, that it did not seem an especially

un•gra•cious

thing to do. She sighed. "Might I trouble you, Miss Murgatroyd, to verify if this is not an

un•gram•mat•i•cal

construction?" "Glad to be of assistance, Mr. Fotheringay," she replied, peering at the paper he offered. They sighed.

regicide — region

reg•i•cide

Now, 007, I am the first to admit that

is, under most circumstances, distasteful
But this

re•gime

cannot be tolerated a day longer than
absolutely necessary. I trust you have
kept up your rigorous physical

reg•i•men

? Good. Your cover will be as one of th

reg•i•ment

of foreign mercenaries that escorts your
target to his daily cricket practice in the
jungle clearing. (I suspect Miss Money-
penny could tell you whether the group

reg•i•men•tals

fit handsomely.) Your contact in the fiel
is code-named

Re•gi•na

and . . . why, yes, she is Irish. I'm afraid
I don't know about any twinkle in her
eye. As ever, 007, your service to Her
Majesty seems to include matters more
than strictly

re•gi•nal

. But that's neither here nor there, I suppos
as long as the assignment is completed
to everyone's satisfaction. At the embassy
our contact is

Reg•i•nald

Watts, the First Secretary. Reliable chap
quite sound. Our best reports are that th

re•gion

is likely to explode if you botch this one
I don't have to tell you, 007, to be careful

195

xanthous — xebec

Behind us, the desert stretched like a searing wave of eternity. How far we'd traveled together! How close we'd grown! And now, our skin

xan•thous

and our faces haggard from our travails, we stumbled the last yards to the city walls. "What place is this, good man?" "Traveler, this be

Xan•thus

, fabled city of beautiful women and handsome men," said the guard. "Hell! We were on our way to Casablanca . . . or was it San José? Hard to remember sometimes," said

Xa•vi•er

Dinwiddie, my companion, shaking out the tattered map. "But how about a drink anyway?" I began. "No time for that now. I see what happened: You got the

x-ax•is

confused with the y-." "The why?" "No, no. The y-axis. Last time I let you plot our course. That's a *man's* job, and you seem to have one

X chromosome

too many, if you ask me," he snapped. The sun beat down like a sadistic conductor. Ahead, through the gates, perhaps salvation awaited. "In fact," I retorted, "nobody asked you,

X.D.

, and I'll thank you to keep your mouth shut." The guard stared. "Speaking of getting your axes mixed up," he said, "is it indelicate to note that there's only *one* of you?" "Well,

Xe   is for Xenon, which I can fathom. But Pb for lead? You gotta admit, that does not compute. With a hey, nonny, nonny. "Don't worry, we've got a nice comfortabl

xe•bec   about to set sail for . . . where did you say you were headed?" "Tipperary, as in it's a long way to, thank you muchly." Behind us, the desert stretched like Jane Fonda.

Abaddon — abbess

Even if one happens to be

A•bad•don , grim angel of hell, one occasionally tires of the wailing dead and the smoky darkness on all sides, ahead and

a•baft one. Even torture grows tiresome. Thus, Abaddon, impulsively streaking from hell, swept down to the ocean and caught a hapless

ab•a•lo•ne in his long-nailed hand. A tasty bite, for a change. "Now, what puny human will

a•ban•don all hope, confronted by oneself?" But to his surprise, the California beach seemed nearly

a•ban•doned . Nary a simple-minded lover of nature? Well, onward to France, where there's sure to be something of interest. Within moments, he was dropping from the sky. A noisy crowd. A placard reading: "

à bas *les juifs*, *les arabes*, *les américains*!" Chants, gesticulations, beatings, turmoil! Abaddon alit, his flames self-snuffing, and turned to the nearest rioter. "Down on your knees before me and

a•base yourself, mortal!" But the sudden appearance of the swarthy, muscular figure with the giant glowing wings hardly seemed to

a•bash

the young man, who sneered and waved a cudgel at him. "Down with the strutting angel!" he shouted. "Down with the aristocracy of supernatural creatures!" Indeed, he seemed disinclined to

a•bate

his vituperation. And when another half-dozen brawny men turned toward Abaddon, enflamed by the first one's rhetoric, it began to seem no

a•bate•ment

was imminent. Three of them carried poles, perhaps broomsticks plucked clean, with sharpened ends. They advanced staunchly, poles held out before them, like a moving

ab•a•tis

. *"Fermez*!" shouted Abaddon, his voice fierce and smoky, like unto a volcano near erupting. But as he began to spread his magnificent wings, an

A battery

struck the back of his head. It was consumed in a sizzle. "Another step forward in your ludicrous soldiering, and I will make this street a bloody

ab•at•toir

! You will heartily wish you were scuttling about in some distant

ab•ax•i•al

land where your only interest would be how to end your miserable existence." Suddenly sirens pierced the air. The first man waved to the fiery angel. "Come with us,

ab•ba

, while the police batter this crowd into pulp. We like very much your style!

Mais oui, come ally with us!" Abaddon hesitated, confused. Join forces? "In whose

ab•ba•cy are we, human? Who dares conjure a mutuality of mortal and immortal? Oneself has not aided humans since joining the Mongols in the sack of Baghdad, pride of the

Ab•bas•sid dynasty." "Then it's time you returned to the fray, old one!" replied the man, showing him into the Renault. It sped down the street. "Oneself admires the human freedom of choice." "Oh, that's an

ab•ba•tial matter, *mon vieux*," replied the man, leading him into the abbey. "We live in the present, doing what our leader says." "And who leads you?" His companion threw open the door. "*Monsieur l'*

ab•bé , we bring an ally for the cause." In the bed, a plump man of saintly demeanor stared. "*Enfin*, Pierre! There is a time and a place . . ." Then the other person in the bed turned to face them. Ah, the

ab•bess , out of her habit. Abaddon nodded. Yes, hypocrisy married to malevolence. Perhaps oneself would deign to lend a mighty hand to their plotting after all.

"Ah . . . before we begin, my dear lady, may I trouble you for a brief

o•ri•en•ta•tion course? I'm afraid I . . ." "Sure thing, sweetie. Which

or•i•fice do you wanna start with?" "Heavens! Where have the days of chivalry gone, when gleaming knights thundered 'neath the

or•i•flamme ?" "Say, mister, you here to talk history or what? I'm tired and I've had a long day and I gotta charge you the

orig. price as quoted, O.K.?" "Egad!" "So what's it to be, bud? You wanna get down and dirty, or do some damn

o•ri•ga•mi instead? Look, it's late and I'm pretty beat." "Forgive me, my fair *fille de joie*. I was just recalling the early church father

Or•i•gen and the apocryphal story of what he did to defeat his unholy urges once and for all." "Well, right here is where it's happening, baby, *this* is the

or•i•gin of it all." "Pretty color, purple. Is that what they call a 'merry widow'? I wonder how such a name was arrived at Well! They're so . . . abundant! Ahem. My

o•rig•i•nal plan was not to get quite so . . . involved, shall we say?" "Sure, you wanna just watch, that's cool. But any kinky stuff, any far-out

o•rig•i•nal•i•ty

with handcuffs or honey costs extra." "Handcuffs? For whom? No, no, really, I think a standard transaction would be most appropriate. I should add that I

o•rig•i•nal•ly

was not planning to participate in the primal act, what one might call the

original sin

, at least according to certain Biblical commentators, who persist in reading Genesis as an oblique representation of . . ." "Sega Genesis, you mean?" "Oh, no! Sometimes these moralistic views

o•rig•i•nate

in feelings of inferiority. It could be lack of status, or belonging to the wrong clubs, or even the inability to pronounce those tricky

o•ri•na•sal

words in French. But surely one must understand that not every stream can be an

O•ri•no•co

– which, by the way, is one of South America's most picturesque rivers. Still, as you may agree with me, sometimes it's the quieter things that appeal most. Take the fluty whistle of the Baltimore

o•ri•ole

, for example, or the steady effulgence of the constellation

O•ri•on

in the night sky during winter months, or . . . Heavens, is she *asleep*?"

man jack — manner

	All right! Listen up, every goddamn shivering
man jack	of you. (And ladies, too, 'scuse the language.) Hell, if this is the best
man•kind	can offer, we're in big trouble. You! Stand up straight, stop drooling! Try to look a little
man•like	, for God's sake, even if you can't look
man•ly	, or I'll kick your butt with my regulation boot — rubber sole,
man-made	uppers — right outta here. That goes for you, too, ma'am! Suck in that tummy! Hell, even Horace
Mann	couldn't teach this bunch! Sure, you waltz into town, thinking you got it made, with your goddamn salaries falling like
man•na	into your laps. No way, José! Let me tell you, one of the last gang ended up in the soup on account of the
Mann Act	, another got his hand caught in the till, and you've all heard about the bozo who had a thing for the
man•ne•quin	! When you ladies and gents march out there in front of all them TV cameras for the first time, let me see just a *bit* of that Congressional
man•ner	, okay? Let's make the nice voters back home feel a *little* proud . . .

"No way! I would never hit anyone with a wet noodle, let alone with something like a

knout ! That sounds nasty, man!" Rex shook his head. His identical twin, Dex, gave him a high five. "I'm with him, dude. I

know there's no way in the world we would do something so uncool and actually hurt someone. I mean, like, that's not our style. I suppose you guys with all these charts and computers have a lot of

know-how about some crazy shit and such, but I think what you're doing is a crock – sorry if I've, like, insulted you or anything, but that's how I feel." At the desk, the professor said, "And you say this

know•ing your country may be at war and that this kind of information might prove vital in the war effort?" He noted they'd worn flip flops even though snow covered the campus. "Hey, man, you may be a genius

know-it-all or something, but you'd just be wasting your time. And besides," added Rex, looking over at Dex, "what's in it for us?" "How about

knowl•edge — about yourselves and about other people. And of course you'd be helping your country." Dex laughed. "Mr. Professor, dude, so if we sit in your lab and tell you we wouldn't hurt nobody, we'd become

knowl•edge•a•ble

or something? That sounds like bull, if you know what I mean, nothing personal you understand." "Yeah, man, if you go ahead and ask anyone, we're

known

as lovers, not fighters." "Dude!" said Dex, giving another high five. "Well, if you're so sure of yourselves, why don't you give it a try?" asked the professor. "Surely neither of you wants to be seen as a

know-nothing

who doesn't pay attention to international affairs and the cutting edge of science." "Cutting edge? Whoa, man, slow down. You got a scientific super-knife? No way!" "You two could be the

known quantity

in this experiment, then – a kind of control group against which we measure the response of others. Identical twins are very useful in the scientific frame-work. . . . And we'd pay." "Oh, yeah! For

Knox

, here we come," said Dex. "Yo, dude, we're closer to

Knox•ville

than to Fort Knox." Dex looked at the elderly professor and shook his head. "Man, he's the slow one in the family. That's why he sticks to checkers instead of playing with a bishop or queen or

knt.

" "Hey, but you've never been near any bishop, and the closest to any queen was seeing Queen Latifah on TV. Oh, and our Queen CDs. So stop spreading these rumors, bro. You want a

205

knuck•le   sandwich?" "And I'll give you a smack right back! My brother was hit in the head with a

knuck•le•ball   in Little League, and he's been missing something upstairs ever since!" "Like, you are so talking through your ass, man. He is, Mr. Professor, dude, 'cause he's got a

knuck•le•bone   where he should have a brain." Dex gestured menacingly at his brother as a stern woman with a chart came to stand beside the professor. "Hey, if I had a

knuck•le•dust•er   , you'd be, like, dead meat!" They laughed and did a high five. "Well, if that's how you feel, thanks for coming by," said the professor. "No problemo, dude." Which was the bigger

knuck•le•head   , wondered the professor. "Ah, Marianne! They just don't make identical twins the way they used to . . . and I fear for our country."

Jackson gave a dry laugh, as dry as his martini. "My dear lady, just because I seem to be admiring your

tor•so   doesn't mean I've committed a

tort   ! If so, half the men in this island's famous casinos would be paupers today." He helped himself to another piece of the

torte   , holding the fork lightly between two fingers. "Apple, of course, but with a dash of brandy, I would say?" "If I wanted to accuse you of being a

tort-fea•sor   , Mr. You Haven't Told Me Your Name, I would certainly be able to find better grounds. My torso is indeed admirable, as that fellow over there with the apparent case of

tor•ti•col•lis   appears to think. He keeps jerking his head around in my direction. Unless," she added after a sip of her drink, "he recognizes me from a Wanted poster." "Not likely. His

tor•tile   hands suggest either that he is desperate for more cash or in despair because he knows he'll never – how do you Americans put it? – get to first base with you. Anothe

tor•til•la   ?" "No, thank you. Interesting cuisine in this nightclub." "Rather. But not, I trust, a

tor•tious   offense?" "Oh, I can't keep up with you. I'm like a dull-witted

tor•toise	in this environment, with all you hares about!" "I beg to differ. In that dress, you look more like a jaguar on the prowl – and we poor chaps appeal to you no more than a
tortoise beetle	would." She laughed and selected another delicacy from the tray. "A compliment, sir – but I sense you're fishing for one in return. I'm to say, 'Oh, just take off those
tortoise shell	glasses and you'll seem a sexy jaguar yourself!' Well, I'm rather tired, so excuse me if I don't respond in kind." He gave a slight bow. "Off to
Tor•to•la	tomorrow with that group of antiques in Bermuda shorts?" This time, her expression was wary. "And how did you know *that*? And don't think you can distract me with an offer of
tor•to•ni	. I see maraschino cherries in it, which I abhor." "*Mi dispiace.* Perhaps the dessert chef had the misfortune of an inferior education." Just then, a handful of brown and tan
tor•tri•cid	moths fluttered by, the dark patterns on their wings resembling – what? The large black eyes of a relentless predator? And when he turned back to her, she was nowhere to be seen. 　　　"It's
Tor•tu•ga	you're thinking of," said the guide, gesturing over the placid water. "Tortuga is the former pirate haven, but where we're heading has a less uproarious past." "I see," she replied. "Ah, the

tor•tu•os•i•ty

of history," said Jackson, appearing beside her at the damp railing. "There may not have been pirate strongholds, but the Dutch and the English ruled Tortola at different times." "Speaking o

tor•tu•ous

things, I thought I'd given you the slip last night, and I took a very twisting path from my hotel. How did you find me?" "Nice outfit. Your school colors?" When she did not respond, he said, "I had to

tor•ture

every ship's captain on the island until I got what I needed." She peered over her sunglasses and sniffed. "I wouldn't put it past you." He smiled. "You seem to regard me as a form of

tor•tu•la

." "I beg your pardon?" "A fungus." "Ah. Well, then, quite accurate. I just hope you won't be growing on *me*." "And that one," said Jackson, sighing, ' will leave alone."
The day,

tor•tur•ous

in some ways because he had worn elegant leather shoes and a blue blazer rather than more "sensible" attire, was very interesting in other ways. As they tramped about the island, she mentione

To•run

, a Polish city, where she still had what she quaintly called a "pen pal" from her semester abroad in Warsaw. "Where did you go to college?" he asked, helping her over a

to•rus

in their path leading back to the powdery white-sand beach. "Nowhere that would interest you, I'm sure." She spoke of her best friend,

To•ry , whose family had several racehorses and – at least at one time – a private jet. "That must have been exciting." "The first flight, perhaps," she said with a shrug. "We flew to

Tos•ca•na for a long weekend our senior year. We'd be more frugal today." "And why is that?" Before answering, she made an elegant gesture worthy of

Tos•ca•ni•ni toward the trio of long-legged shore birds ahead of them. "Because all of us have smarter things to do with our money now, what there is of it." "Investments and that sort of

tosh , I suppose? Probably wise." "What do *you* know about being wise, Mr. Jackson?" she shot back with a

toss of her head. "You've got sand in your expensive shoes!" "Ah, yes, not the best pair for walking on the beach. They'll think I'm a

toss•pot or a lunatic." "Or something worse – a ridiculous gold digger," she said with a wry smile. "It's probably a

toss•up , I would say." She looked out over the bay. "Quite calm, isn't it?" he said, nodding toward the water. "Nothing tempest-

tost about it this afternoon." "Throwing in some Shakespeare for my benefit?" He laughed. "You seem a little suspicious, Miss Perloff – whereas *I'm* just hungry. Do you think they'd have a

tos•ta•da   on this British island for virgins?" It wa[s] her turn to laugh. "We could ask that

tot   in the blue shirt where to find something edible," he said. "Well, I'm more inter-ested in a nice little

tot   with something alcoholic in it. I hope you don't think I'm wicked, Mr. Jackson. "Not at all. I'm sure if I had a

tot.   of all the terrible things you've done over the years, I still wouldn't consider you wicked. Not with your generous spirit and obvious concern for people." "And you know these things with

to•tal   certainty?" she asked, slipping off her sandals and edging closer to the water. "My father might not agree. He saw

total depravity   where you see generosity. That's why h[e] structured his will the way he did." "Hi[s] will? Interesting." "Yes, isn't it. At leas[t] to some people." He tsked, then said, "I'm afraid I'm not a

to•tal•i•sa•tor   who bothers with that rubbish. And wh[o] can think of money in such surroundings?" He studied his shoes, as if contemplatin[g] what would happen if he took them off. "No, with a

to•tal•is•tic   view, one has to take all these different things into account, and then one is more likely to find one's balance." "As opposed to finding someone *else's* balance?" She laughed. "My rather

to•tal•i•tar•i•an   father took a more focused view of life.

"And that was Mr. Perloff?" "Yes, it was. I suspect you know his first name." "I suspect you suspect me of . . . impure motives." "Given the

to•tal•i•ty   of our experience today, I think I have every right to suspect you, Mr. Jackson – if that is indeed your name. Oh, it's not so obvious, but I can tell you're adding everything up like a seasoned

to•tal•i•za•tor   , estimating what my clothing cost, what my rings are worth, what I paid for my hotel room and such. Well, Mr. Jackson,

to•tal•ize   away. Draw your conclusions. Decide whether I'm worth the pursuit – or is it all over, now that I've unmasked you as a cold-blooded

to•tal•iz•er   ? And I'm quite sure you know all about how my family's money is now mine after years of legal hassling. What more could I want now than a well-spoken hunk with a British accent?" "You

to•tal•ly   misjudge me, Miss Perloff," he said, smiling. "I'm no dangerous con man like the notorious Crispin Sims. Yes, I know some of the particulars of your situation, but not with

total recall   . That's why I brought some things with me," he said, pulling out a vial from his jacket. She shrunk back. "Poison? You're going to *kill* me?" "No, no, it's a precaution – it's

to•ta•quine   , an anti-malarial powder. I have every interest in keeping you alive – and so does my employer." She frowned, trying to

tote   up all the clues in her head. "Who –
MI6? The K.G.B.? My ex-husband's
lawyers? *People* magazine?" "No, Miss
Perloff. Fortunately, I had the foresight to

tote   a few relevant papers with me. I think
you'll find them worthwhile, especially
after I learned about your generous
bequest to the orphanage on one of the
nearby islands. I can

tote   your bag for you while you take a look
at them." "No, thank you," she responded
hugging her

tote bag   closer, still eyeing the vial. "Well," he
continued, giving his most sincere smile
"it's a detailed plan for making a major
gift to your alma mater. Miss Perloff,
one doesn't need a

tote board   to see how expensive a college education
is today, how vital it is for less wealthy
students. Your gift would allow us – "
But she stared at him as if he were a
creature who'd climbed down from a

to•tem   pole. "With a sizable endowment, the in
terest itself would . . ." She gave a shriek
and started running back to the path.
"Miss Perloff, we know how much you
treasured your four years at . . ."

lycanthrope — Lycia

Oh, they called it the Age of Social Correctness, when every conceivable form of human creed, race, and behavior was accepted, but Horst knew how shallow that view was. As a well-mannered

ly•can•thrope

with a hardly placeable accent and a touch of raspiness when he spoke excitedly, Horst had learned that some topics –

ly•can•thro•py

, for example – were off limits. And yet he had a pedigree none of his acquaintances could come near! He had shone in the Parisian

ly•cée

and had never been suspected in the disappearance of that *espèce d'idiot* Jean-Paul. Indeed, Justine had laughingly said he could have sat at the feet of the old philosophers of the

Ly•ce•um

, given Horst's knowledge of certain arcane volumes. It was one of his few regrets that poor Justine had glimpsed him during the full moon. He had buried her under a tree - what was it, a

ly•chee

? It may have been only his imagination, but he believed the next year's fruit was more brilliantly red than before. Ah, no one knew his sentimental side! He could not approach the

lych•gate

of Justine's church, not while the burial was in progress. But later, when dark-

214

ness had fallen, he had left a bunch of colorful

lych•nis coronaria outside the gate to her family's villa. Oh, he tried, he dearly tried to follow all the rules of modern humanity. Hath not a werewolf affections? Constrain beyond mortal understanding? In

Ly•ci•a , where his ancient tribe once lived, they were – let us be frank – savages! But those days are gone. Well, take your miraculous pills, turn the lights off, climb into bed. Hope for the best.

reiterate —— rejuvenate

Loss, dejection, a feeling like unto death – this, I must

re•it•er•ate , is the literary life. The evidence is clear. Each evening, after dragging myself home, I check my mail. A-ha! An envelope, self-addressed to yours truly. At once, I

reive the envelope and start to unfold the editor's considered verdict. Deep breath before reading. . . . Damnation! This one opts to

re•ject my crafted conte of passion and intrigue in the Rare Book Room, and in my trembling fingers the

rejection slip burns. Oh, this must be the closest to despair a body can feel on this earth. I swear the hordes of devils are gathering to

re•joice , for another lost soul is staggering on his way. And as their hateful

re•joic•ing wells up in my ears, I weigh the other envelope. What's the point of opening it? But after a moment, I do. . . . Good God! Can it be? Is it true? At once, I

re•join the human race: it's an acceptance! My double sestina on the utter hopelessness of life has been bought (at something like .037 cents a word), and I can now

re•join   to all the doubters that talent and tenacity
do indeed win in the end. As someone
once said – well, maybe *I* said it – life is
the supreme

re•join•der   to death. There *is* a meaning to all this
struggling; there *is* a purpose to my
existence; literature *can*

re•ju•ve•nate   one's tattered spirit. . . . But what's this?
An e-mail has just arrived. Another
editorial fiend has turned me down? Damn
it, I'm gonna blow up his bleeping Porsche

badly — baggy

bad•ly

Cecile: pale, ethereal, almost unearthly. "I love her madly," declared Watts, chin firm. "Odd. I would have said you love her ," responded Compton with a sneer. "I can assure you that *she* has no sense of your supposed passion. Do us all a favor and get thee hence – the hencer, the better." "And leave her for a

bad•man

like you, Compton? Ha!" Compton shook his head. "Well, then, if you won't listen to reason, how about an appeal to honor? We'll play for the right to her hand. Baccarat?" "I prefer

bad•min•ton

," said Watts, bemoaning the muscles that Compton's well-tailored suit did little to conceal. But Watts knew nothing about gambling, so racquets it would be. They moved to the lawn. As

bad-tem•pered

as Compton was, he could play with patience – and cunning. By the end Watts was damp with sweat and pink with humiliation. "Here," said Compton, tossing him a well-thumbed

Bae•de•ker

. "I beg your pardon?" "Well, seeing as you lost your bid, I thought surely you'd prefer to leave the country rather than loiter about while I win Cecile's heart. Isn't there somewhere called

Baf•fin

in Canada? You'd be able to cool your heels there – and the rest of you as well." He sniffed. "From what I hear, it's a nation of losers. You'd be right at home."

Sailing into

Baffin Bay   one month later, Watts told himself he would only return to England once he had hardened his heart to his loss – or hatched a plan to win Cecile's love. He found a small cabin on

Baffin Island   . Canada would make him a man – or would break him. He denied himself his daily chocolates easily enough, but how to keep from looking at her photograph? That would

baf•fle   him until the end of time. What a sad smile! Still, he knew he'd have to develop his strength to be able to face down Compton. So he shoveled snow; chopped down trees; shoveled snow; hauled

bag   after bag of flour from the trading post to his cabin; shoveled snow. He ached, but he knew it would do him good. When the worst snowstorm of the season came, he had to use

ba•gasse   to light his lantern. When his food supplies ran down, he tried seal fat, seasoned with salt and paprika. He realized he would have to learn what was essential and what was a mere

bag•a•telle   . Then came the letter from his cousin in England, with a gossip column announcing that Cecile and Compton were to vacation in New York. It might just as well be Pago Pago or

Bag•dad , thought Watts, who promptly sought to distract himself by plunging into high-minded studies by Trevelyan and

Bage•hot . But then he reconsidered. It would be his last chance to see her – and to see whether there remained any hope. He trudged into town on snowshoes and . . . "And you call this a

ba•gel ? Delightful." Watts sauntered along Broadway. He peered up at the skyscrapers. He admired the women passing by – Anglo blonde, Latino brunette, Asian vixen, African queen. He bought a

bag•ful of tortilla chips. He tried a steak house that made him forget the meals of yesteryear. And only then did he meet Cecile and Compton in their hotel lobby, surrounded by their expensive

bag•gage . "Leaving so soon?" he asked, offering them a chip. Odd: had Cecile always been so pale, so insubstantial? She, in turn, gasped, scarcely recognizing the well-toned figure before her. "Are you

bagged , old chap?" asked Compton warily. "Oh, no, just enjoying myself." He shook his head. "What the deuce was I thinking, sticking myself in the Canadian snows! I could get a job today at Gristedes,

bag•ging groceries." His gaze followed a buxom young thing. "Whoa, mama!" "Reggie? Are you feeling quite right?" "Think my trousers are too

bag•gy , Cecile? They seem to like tight jeans here. Oh, and bon voyage."

zoot suit — zowie

I was grumbling, not for the first time. Writing a tale would be so much easier if all the letters of the alphabet were used equally. It's really hard to use "x" or . . . Then I saw them, each wearing a

zoot suit

, faces with a peculiar greenish pallor. How they managed to find their way to my study so silently – and without a key to the front door – was beyond me. "My name is

Zor•ach

. Welcome." He stood about four feet high. "It's not customary for people barging into someone's house to say 'welcome,'" I replied testily. My testiness increased when I glimpsed his

zo•ri

under his pegged trousers, revealing very ugly toes. "I don't allow flip flops in my home." "Flip flops?" "Thongs. Whatever you want to call them. Even those Japanese ones." "Well, I'll be a ravin

zor•ille

," said the second uninvited visitor. "They told us these were the latest thing in Earthwear – in desirable style, I mean." He bowed stiffly. "We are from Persia. I am

Zorn

, second in com –, uh, boon companion to Zorach, whom I know from when we were knee high to a . . ." He raised a bristly eyebrow. "A kudu?" "Yes, exactly!' "Talked recently to

Zo•ro•as•ter

?" I asked, already having some doubts. "He is friend to you?" "Oh, intimate. He and Abélard and Heloise and I used to run around like there was no tomorrow.'

"Excellent man you is no doubt then

Zo•ro•as•tri•an , my recommendation is," said the third visitor, who seemed a little younger. "We learned that Mister Zoroaster taught the doctrine of

Zo•ro•as•tri•an•ism , by which is understood that existence holds two ultimate forces, Ahura Mazda and Ahriman. My name is

Zor•ri•lla , at your indentured service." Well, I needed three "foreigners" interrupting my precious time for writing as much as I needed a terrible case of herpes

zos•ter , but my middle name is Gracious Host. "So . . . who are you looking for? I'm afraid I don't have much to offer." "But you are author of the Tales from Webster's? Known to be truly

Zou•ave , with implacable manners." "Oh, you mean *suave*!" I waved modestly. "But how could you know about the Tales? They haven't even been published yet!" "Our copy comes from

Zoug , Switzerland, the Golden Chamois Edition, with engravings by Dubois," said Zorach. "Surely you know it!" I could only stare. "Hellation, did we set the Time Questor wrong again? Oh,

zounds !" "How many years in the future?" I asked, reaching shakily for my desk. "Wait, it's better not to know." I sighed. "But in the meantime, there's only one word for this situation:

zow•ie !" "No, thank you," replied Zorn. "Never before lunch."

par•a•mount
par•a•mour
Pa•ra•ná
pa•rang
par•a•noi•a
par•a•noid
par•a•nor•mal
par•a•nymph
par•a•pet
par•aph
par•a•pher•na•li•a
par•a•phrase

John Shea was born in Rome, the son of a Foreign Service Officer. He graduated from Columbia University, then earned a Ph.D. at the University of Pennsylvania. There, he won Penn's awards for playwriting and for poetry. After that, he worked at Penn for many years as an editor and writer. He may be the only person to have published stories in both *Partisan Review* and *Alfred Hitchcock's Mystery Magazine*. His story "The Real World" received an honorable mention from *Writer's Digest,* was published in *Columbia Magazine,* and was later performed as part of Writing Aloud, a program of InterAct Theatre Company of Philadelphia. He won second prize in the Philadelphia City Paper fiction competition with a story set in Colonial Philadelphia; it included witchcraft and a cameo by B. Franklin. Other stories have appeared in *The Twilight Zone Magazine, The Café Irreal, Literal Latte,* and elsewhere.